NOW AND AT THE HOUR

BESS KERCHER

This is a work of fiction. Names, characters, businesses, places, events, locales, and incidents are either the products of the author's imagination or used in a fictitious manner.

Copyright © 2020 by Bess Kercher

ISBN: 978-1-7355601-6-8

Kercher, Bess.
Now and at the Hour.

Edited by: Monika Dziamka

Published by Warren Publishing
Charlotte, NC
www.warrenpublishing.net
Printed in the United States

For Sheri

"And all the time we talked you seemed to see
Something down there to smile at in the dust."
–Robert Frost, "Meeting and Passing"

The boy wants to look away, but he can't take his eyes off the beautiful black-and-white beast rolling in the surf. It's battered against the rocks with each wave, then dragged back out, only to come tumbling forward again. At first, he can't tell what exactly he's seeing, but when the sun hits upon a dorsal fin, he realizes it's a young shark.

A crowd has started to gather at the shore. People pull out their phones and begin to take pictures and videos. Every time the waves retreat, the boy hopes they'll be strong enough to force the shark back to where it belongs. Instead the opposite is happening—the shark gets closer and closer to the shore. One thing is clear: this animal is suffering.

The boy doesn't have a plan. He's not really thinking. He slips out of his shoes and gets rid of his phone. The water is so cold, and the shark ... is a shark. None of that matters though. All he knows is there's no way he's going to just stand there and watch something die.

SUMMER

CHAPTER 1
TRICKS AND LIES

The craziest thing isn't that I had decided to post my most embarrassing moment on YouTube. The craziest thing is that it had been Mom's idea. Then again, that's the way me and Mom usually roll. Except in this case we're talking about a skateboarding video, and that can be a little different. It's probably the only major thing we don't have in common. I don't take it personally though. Flint and Jabari have the same deal as me.

All of our moms hate that we board. Well, maybe hate's a strong word, but they all worry a lot about the fact that we board and we do it on the streets of San Francisco, which I admit has really steep hills (so sweet!)—but that's not our fault. We live here! Are we supposed to get on a plane and fly to someplace really flat and boring every time we want to skateboard? I don't think so. We've agreed to wear helmets when we do it (which is pretty annoying, but I get it) and to mostly stick to the parks, but only certain parts of the park, and not at night. And always with someone else. It had been a real pain to hammer out these details.

But once we had, I was typically good to go without getting a lot of grief. And I've never given Mom a real reason to shut it down. Until earlier today.

I had tried to sneak past her this morning through the back door and over to the bathroom to grab a towel to stop the blood, but there was no way to avoid the kitchen, and that's where she was parked. I pulled the sleeve of my hoodie until it wrapped over my whole hand, covering my arm completely. I could feel the wetness seep into the sleeve. I stretched the whole mess tight around the scrapes on my stomach. Tears burned my eyes when it brushed against the skin, but I shut that right down. I set my face like normal except with a little smile. It wasn't one of those times that I wanted to lie to her, even though there was no choice now. It was more that I didn't want her to feel bad about boarding. And okay ... I really didn't want her to feel bad about me.

A long time ago I hadn't cared about that. I couldn't because I was little. There were problems that you might say were my fault. Or if you were Sister, you'd say it's not fair to talk about fault because of all the stuff that had happened to us. These are details that aren't important. This is: I hurt my mom a lot. It's my worst thing.

It won't ever happen again.

So, I tried to bust past her as fast as I could, like I really had to pee. I would've made it, too—she had her nose all in the newspaper and her coffee, which is her favorite thing in life. And at least I'm really good at getting the story solid when I'm hurt. It's like I do the opposite of panic. Like when the basketball had come flying across the gym and landed weird and hard on my finger. I knew then that the drama was going to be too much for her, so I told my first No Worries Little White Lie, that I just liked wearing skate gloves all the time. I kept the bandage underneath, out of sight. She never actually knew that it was broken. One day we held our hands palm to palm to see how big mine was compared to hers, and her eyes landed on the crooked finger and got real wide. She looked at me and was quiet, except to close her fingers over mine and squeeze them a little. She never asked. I never told.

As I went past, she grabbed my shirt from the back and pulled it toward her. I'm betting this was for a quick kiss on the cheek, which I usually don't fight, but this time the pulling ripped the fabric from my cuts. The shock of it threw me totally off my game. I yelled and she jumped and knocked her coffee over and let out a little scream—and then she saw the blood and let out a big one.

"Albert Davidson! Oh my God, what in the world?" She pulled the shirt away, which hurt like heck, but I worked hard to keep my face straight. She looked me up and down with her eyes going back and forth a million miles an hour. Finally, she grabbed my arm and dragged me toward the kitchen sink. She snatched the dishtowel and wet it and then pressed it to my stomach while I yelped.

"Mom! It's nothing. I'm fine." I could tell she was getting upset. I looked her right in the eye. "We were just pulling some branches away from the playhouse we're building for J's sisters, and I got scraped up. Dr. Pahlavi said it's nothing."

There. That covered all of our bases. She loves when I hang out with super-nice Jabari. Bonus points 'cause his mom's a doctor and can sign off on my status. This NWLWL was super legit.

Except she saw right through it. Her eyes narrowed, and then she closed them for a second. My stomach flipped a little. When she spoke, she nailed it. No one could say my mom's not smart.

"I'm thinking maybe you need to back off the board."

No! Switch gears. "Well, if it doesn't kill you, it will make you stronger, right?" I said, thinking of her favorite Kelly Clarkson song. Maybe I could make her laugh. Mom loves Kelly Clarkson. For some reason that song was on constant rotation over here recently.

Mom rolled her eyes. She held onto her side in a weird way and winced a little bit. That seemed pretty funny since there was so much drama about what had happened to me. So I jumped all over it. "You look like you feel worse than me! I'm thinking maybe you need to back off the coffee." As soon as it was out of my mouth, I wanted to suck it back in. I really wasn't trying to talk back. I looked at Mom closely. She squeezed her side another time and then took a deep breath. Then she squinted at me and set her mouth in this way she does when we goof around. *Whew!* I relaxed a little.

"All right. Maybe I should, skater boy. As much as I love it, I'd give it a rest if it would make this crap go away," she said and squeezed her side again.

Lucky for Mom—and probably me, too, come to think of it, since I live with her—coffee doesn't have anything to do with pulled muscles.

"And that's the difference between you and me. I don't suppose you would ever *not* board, right?" She said this in a really cool way, not a lecture-y way like she thought it was dumb that I like it so much.

She knew the answer—she didn't really have to even ask that question. I shook my head hard, pressing the cool cloth on my skin. Give up boarding? Never! In fact, that was my number one goal for the summer. To keep getting better and to maybe one day get sponsored.

"Well, I hope whatever caused this was worth it," Mom said.

I felt my face get red. She raised her eyebrows like a question.

"Did you record it?"

When I didn't answer, she set her lips together into a firm line. "Let me see it."

I wanted so many things at once. I wanted to disappear in a flash. I wanted the phone to explode in my hand. I wanted to come up with a killer NWLWL that would Mr. Clean Magic Eraser that crease on her forehead. Even more than all that, I wanted to tell her. I wanted to say, *You won't believe it—it went waaaay to the bad, but before that, it was amazing!* I wanted to tell her that on my board, wild and stupid, going straight for the crazy, I'm totally free.

But I didn't say anything. I opened my phone to the clip. I watched her face as she watched the video. I heard the muffled sound of trashcans dragging across the pavement. Her eyebrows went up, and I knew she was at the part where we were balancing the pool noodle we'd found sticking out of the dumpster across the tops of the cans. In the background you could hear the clicking of balls hitting rackets and people laughing and somebody's music blaring in Dolores Park.

From the phone, the sound of my wheels whirred on the pavement. Mom smiled as the sound stopped when I popped my board and kicked it up—I'd caught air better than ever before and landed the sweetest Ollie. It was so sick. But then her face set in a sort of bracing way, and I knew she saw me zooming toward the cans. Then the hard scrape right before the jump. My cuts tingled as I thought about what came next, and I looked hard at Mom. I thought about grabbing the phone from her hands, but it was too late. I heard the sound of my feet leaving the board and then nothing for the few seconds when I was suspended in air over the noodle—I really had nailed that part—but the landing was the major fail. If I'd been a cartoon, the word SPLAT would've been across the frame.

Mom's hand went over her mouth. I could see she was biting her lip. This was bad. I took a deep breath and reached for the phone. But before I could exhale, the whole scene flipped. I peered hard into her face to make sure I was seeing what I thought I was seeing.

Mom wasn't crying. She was laughing.

"Oh, Albie," she said, trying to look serious. But she couldn't hold it in. "I'm sorry. It's just ..." she looked back down at the screen and then just kinda lost it. Talk about LOL. "This ... this ... is *awesome*."

CHAPTER 2
THE FAVE

I let out my breath. It was cool that she wasn't mad. I wasn't sure how to feel about her laughing at me. But when she replayed the video again and my brain wasn't overloaded with possible upcoming punishments, I felt the corners of my mouth twitch when I got to the bad part. It was funny, actually.

And awesome, no doubt. Because I probably should've ended up in my room without privileges, but instead, once I'd stopped bleeding and changed my shirt, I could still head out to meet Flint and J. The Three Amigos weren't going to be disbanded the first week of summer even though I'd messed up. Lucky for us, Mom was still on the laptop laughing at my newly posted video on YouTube.

I showed up first at The Fave and grabbed our second-favorite spot on the patio out front. Before long I saw Flint coming down the street. I knew him from pretty far away because he's played Pop Warner football since he was, like, eight years old, and he looks like it. We're the same height and both pretty strong, but Flint's arm is the size of my leg. I watched him flip his helmet off with one quick movement. He keeps his hair really short, almost like a military cut. That's pretty unusual for a boarder, at least one from around here, but being unexpected is part of what makes Flint who he is.

He started whooping it up as soon as he saw me. "Al-bee! Albert Christian Davidson in da house!" he yelled, squinting his blue eyes and using his cupped fist like a megaphone. "What's goin' on, son?"

I smiled like I always do when I hear Flint. Some people think the way he talks sounds weird, but my mom's from South Carolina too. Her accent isn't as thick as Flint's, but it has a similar twang. When she's on the phone with my Uncle Wood, though, it's like Flint's accent times ten thousand. She gabs away, always telling stories and jokes about where they're from. As she gets more and more Southern-sounding, she draws out his name: "Ellllllllllwoooood." She stays on the phone forever and laughs the whole time.

"Just trying to keep from starving while I'm waiting ten years for you to get here," I said, because that's the kind of thing that's fun to do with Flint, just to keep it going.

"Dang, well okay then. Sorry. Just thought I'd give you a little time to get the all-clear from the Urgent Care." He looked hard at my bandaged arm, and I felt my face start to get red. The video of my smacking into the pavement burned in my brain. I looked like such an idiot in that footage. Maybe I should break the rule about always boarding with someone else.

He punched me lightly. "Hey. No worries, Albie."

He jerked his shirtsleeve back and flexed his arm. A long scar cut across his muscle. Flint loves the proof of his running back injury—he jokes about getting "2014 Optimist Bowl Champions" tattooed across it.

"That jump was everything. I'm serious. Like Abraham Lincoln said, 'No pain, no gain.' Battle scars, baby!"

"Yeah. Okay." After a family trip to DC, Flint's been way into President Lincoln. He gives him credit for almost every important saying or idea that he likes. Whatever.

Flint grabbed a menu from the stand as if we didn't already know exactly what we were going to order. He looked out over 18th Street. "Where the heck is G.I. J?"

Just then we saw Jabari jogging up to the parking lot, his board tucked under one arm. If you were going to design an identical twin for Flint, it would be Jabari—on opposite day. Jabari has shaggy, jet-black hair that's cut with long layers across his face. "Bieber-ed," as Flint would say. He has big brown eyes like me but with really thick dark lashes. Which may sound weird for me to notice, but they're so thick, they're really one of the first things you see when you look at him.

J's pretty humble. He's quick to make fun of himself, joking about his hair and his skinny legs and his huge brain. He never acts embarrassed about how close he is to his grandparents and how he's into them being Persian. (I'm into all the cool art from Iran that the Pahlavis have at their house.) Flint started calling him "G.I. J" as a joke after Jabari refused to play Call of Duty with him. Chill Jabari had never really liked war games, even when we were little kids and would play with Flint's G.I. Joe soldier action figures. It probably seems crazy to some people that we would call quiet Jabari something that sounds like a military fighter. Maybe especially that I would, because of what happened to my dad. But given that his other nickname is Bambi, G.I. J just cracks us up.

"Jah-bah-*ree*! What the heck's goin' on, brotha?" Flint said, reaching his hand out to fist-bump Jabari. "We were about to start without you, man. Did they have a casting call for *America's Next Top Model* today or somethin'?"

"Aw, sorry, guys. It takes a lot of work to look this good," Jabari said. He ran his hand through his hair and pushed the thick waves back. Then turned red. Jabari has a hard time taking a compliment, even a joke one he makes himself.

We all laughed and walked past the old, banged-up wooden picnic tables to the order window on the side. I was excited there wasn't a line today, although The Fave usually cranks it out pretty fast. Jabari ordered first and just got a Coke, which was weird. Then I got my favorite—two corn dogs with large onion rings and a banana milkshake.

Flint was last and drummed his fingers against the counter under the ORDER HERE sign and said something that made the lady who was ringing us up laugh. Then he ordered his usual, a burger platter all the way with bacon, ketchup, chili, slaw, pickles, mustard, onions, and fried jalapeños with a side of ranch.

Jabari leaned against one of the thick metal poles holding up the roof over the patio, picking at the peeling red paint and shaking his head as Flint put his order in. He pinched his mouth in a weird way. Flint noticed.

"What's the deal, Bambi? You on a diet? You're a lean, mean green bean as it is," he said, with a nod to Jabari's dark green sweatshirt.

"I just don't know how you eat that much food, Bobo. It seems a little toxic."

Flint smiled when J said his nickname. Juan had been his name last year in Spanish. Juan Bobo—Juan the Fool—was what mean Señor Smith had called him when he came to class late and had to come back in at lunch to clean out the desks. This happened a lot because Flint had Spanish first period and was super challenged in the mornings and usually tardy.

"Ah! *Excellente,*" Señor Smith would bellow as Flint busted in late again. "*Clase,* please say good morning to Juan Bobo, who has so kindly decided to *finally* join us!"

"*Buenos días,* Juan Bobo," the class would say. So now whenever one of us does something dumb, we call it a Juan Bobo and laugh it off. I think it's very solid that Flint turned something embarrassing into something cool.

"Uh huh. I know you usually prefer the lighter side, California boy. But not even an avocado BLT today? I don't know how you can be here and *not* eat."

"Yeah, well. I'm just not feeling it today." Jabari's eyes rested on something for just a second. He seemed to catch himself and straightened his face, but not before Flint followed his gaze to the sign posted in the window. It was the restaurant score. The Fave got an eighty-nine.

I could see this info play across Flint's mind the same way it played across mine. Maybe not the greatest, but not a disaster. I took a sip of my milkshake and held the sugary coldness on my tongue. Yeah, we were good.

But not so much for Jabari—although I could tell he wasn't loving that he was busted on this front.

"No *way*. You aren't eating because The Fave got less than an A? Ya know, not everybody's as super smart as you, J. Some of us aspire to a B plus." Flint took a big bite out of his burger. Pickles and mustard fell out of the bun and slid down his chin.

Jabari wrinkled his nose. I had to admit, that wasn't the most appetizing sight. But my corn dog was *gooood*.

"You're probably right," he said. "But don't you wonder just a little bit why they'd lose points?"

"Nope," Flint said, dragging his jalapeño fries through the cardboard tub of ranch.

"Like, would that be for rotten food? Or for not cleaning things, right? Rat crap in the kitchen?"

Flint and I both stopped midchew. Gross.

Jabari had twisted around toward the restaurant report card as he was talking, but when he turned back to us and saw our faces, he looked startled.

"Aw, man. Sorry! Seriously. I'm sure it's ... nothing."

We sat there for a moment, unconvinced. Jabari reached around and grabbed a handful of my onion rings and stuffed them in his mouth. He swallowed and then smiled really big. He jumped out of his seat and jogged toward the counter again. I wasn't sure if he was just too starving to not give in to The Fave or if he didn't want to ruin our lunch and so was diving in. It could be either, knowing Jabari. But he did look pretty happy when he returned with his standard BLT and root beer float.

Hanging out with my best friends was pretty sweet. When we got up to go, I was ready to mark this up as a perfect day, even with my early morning crash-and-burn. Then I noticed a group of guys coming down Van Ness. But what went through my mind when I saw them was *gang of guys,* because leading the pack front and center was the always-annoying Pat McBee.

I don't know for sure what had happened to Pat to make him so foul, but I guess it must've been pretty tragic. Ugly seems to be his default mode. For as long as I can remember, Pat's always been a pain, but once he got spring fever, he was really out of control. I couldn't wait for school to end so I wouldn't have to deal with him. Or so I thought.

At first seeing Pat made me worry. Then the fact that I was worried made me mad. I could feel the anger starting inside, and I closed my eyes. I imagined walking into a room with bright lights, and then I flipped the switch so that the room got dark and I calmed down. I forced that nothing feeling as I watched Pat's smirk when he saw us. He said something to the other guys, and they all laughed.

As they got closer to us, I could see Jabari tense up. He was clenching and unclenching his fists. Not in a fighting way but in a nervous way. Flint worked a wad of gum around in his mouth and squinted his eyes at Pat, with his arms crossed on his chest. I kept my face really calm and blank. My heart was starting to pound. I took a deep breath.

"What's up, ladies?" Pat said loudly, like he was on stage somewhere. His two buddies smirked. Flint scowled and rolled his eyes as if to say, *Is that the best you got?* Jabari kind of laughed and shook his head. Pat turned to face J. His eyes narrowed until they rested on Jabari's Vine board.

"Hey, Aladdin, I didn't know the Taliban let you girls skateboard these days. Shouldn't you be covering your face with some scarf? You're an embarrassment, man."

I could feel my eyes getting wide. As Pat's friends laughed, I saw Jabari's face get red. I let those comments sink in. Pat managed to say a bunch of really stupid things in just a few words.

The fact that the Pahlavis are Catholic like the rest of us doesn't matter at all. I've seen Jabari have to deal with this before. I knew he'd never get into it to set the record straight. To make some huge scene to say he isn't Muslim or isn't Arab or whatever Pat was getting at is just not cool. It'd be like saying those things are bad. Which they aren't.

Jabari stood there saying nothing. My eyes met his, and he looked miserable. Flint seemed ramped up, sort of leaning back and forth, his leg muscles tensing with each move. This was not good.

Pat pushed the sleeves of his army jacket up over his elbows—maybe it's easier to punch someone that way. It sorta surprised me to remember that Pat and I both had dads in the military. Something came over me when I thought of my dad. I got really focused. All of a sudden, I remembered a picture that had dropped from Pat's notebook when he was getting his math folder out of his locker on the last day of school. The lie came fast then.

"We don't know anything about the Taliban, but J's skateboarding's good enough for Cousin Kim K." I stared right into his eyes really strong and did not look away.

Pat blinked. His face got red. "Kim who?" he said, but his voice was kind of funny.

"Kardashian, man! Jabari and his moves are going to end up on her Insta any day now."

"Davidson, you're so full of crap," Pat said, but I could see he was thinking about it. Jabari does look a bit like the Kardashian clan.

"Nope. Just skateboarding with a celebrity. I thought that might interest you."

Pat's face told me that he knew that I knew about the Kim pictures in his notebook. He looked mad and didn't say anything else. I think he realized that I was messing with him—but also that I wasn't going to tell his secret.

"Whatever, losers. Come on, let's get out of here. The food sucks." Pat turned around, and his crew fell in place behind him.

Once they were out of earshot, Flint started laughing and pounding me on the back. "What the heck was that?" he asked. "I mean, don't get me wrong, you rock, but ... the Kardashians? I don't get it."

I looked at Jabari and could tell that he also didn't get it. Then again, maybe he did. I hoped he wasn't mad. It was kind of like I did what Pat was doing about Jabari's looks, but I did it for a good reason. Did that make it okay?

"Listen, whatever that was about, thanks, man," Jabari said. He looked like he really meant it. I knew we were good. "But you know the Kardashians are Armenian, not Persian."

"Whaaaat?" Flint smacked his head and started laughing. "Dude! Don't embarrass yourself. I'm not even going to ask how in the heck you know that!"

I guessed it was because of J's sisters, who were obsessed with the E! channel, but I just laughed with the guys. I was glad things had turned around. I thought of when I had felt that calm come over me and I knew what to do. When I was younger, Mom had always said my dad was with me, watching me from heaven. There were times when I thought so, and times when I didn't—but I knew he had been helping me then. Today I knew that it was possible to be gone in most ways, but to somehow still be here just the same.

CHAPTER 3
RED, WHITE, AND BLUE

I woke up to the sound of my mom laughing, her voice bouncing off the walls through the whole house. It's not a given that my mom would sound happy like that today. It's July Fourth. Which is a pretty fun holiday for most people, the birthday of our nation and all. My birthday is also this week, and I'm pretty pumped about it. But if someone in your family had been in the military and they died fighting in a war, July Fourth makes you feel sad too. Proud, sorry, sad, and mad. For me the Fourth of July is like every emotion you could think about rolled into one confusing mess.

I opened my eyes and remembered it was the Fourth and started having all those thoughts. Then it was just good to hear my mom laugh so loud. And that could only mean one person was on the other end of the phone.

I think my Uncle Wood has to be my mom's favorite person in the whole world. Well, maybe next to me. At least that's what she'd say. But even I can't make her laugh like that. Or act so silly. There must've been something about growing up together in Berks, South Carolina, that has bonded them forever. And made them a little weird. Or as my mom would say, "colorful." Which is a nicer way to describe it.

Uncle Wood lives back in South Carolina now, in Charleston. He runs an art gallery there. He reps a couple of really wild artists and still has some good friends in the business here in San Francisco. Which is awesome. It means he can get back out to the West Coast and see us a few times a year. The house where we live used to be his a long time ago. It's pretty cool when he comes back to hang out here with us.

He's the reason I like to draw. Even when I was little, he used to always give me art supplies and strange pieces of real art. Some of them came from all across the world. Some were made from wood and metal and things you'd never think could make anything interesting or pretty. But when you put them all together they looked a million times better than before. Even stuff that was actual trash could be made into something beautiful.

But the coolest part of Uncle Wood being in the art world is that he sells paintings from my favorite artist. Oris Hart was an okay painter—he did pictures of fruit and flowers and kind of boring stuff. But then something happened, and he started painting really different. Really wild, colorful landscapes that are super fierce looking.

A lot of his paintings have cool trees in them. That is what made me first notice them at Uncle Wood's gallery. I was a lot younger then, but I saw the tree in the painting and I walked up to it and stood very still right in front of it. I've always had something about trees, ever since

I used to climb one with my dad at our favorite park when I was little. It had always been our special thing. It became even more so when my dad said goodbye to me through that tree. I know that sounds crazy and weird. But I really don't care what anyone thinks about it.

Whether or not Uncle Wood had connected all of that in his mind when I saw the painting, I don't know. He had known about when my dad's tree fell, so maybe. Or maybe he just liked that I liked it, and so he wanted me to be able to take it in and really get into it. He told me about Oris Hart and how he had been in a terrible accident and almost died, and how he woke up instead and began painting these amazing pictures. And ever since then he became my favorite painter, and I decided that art was very solid. It became something I would do and protect, even if other kids made fun of it or if nobody else thought it was cool.

So when I heard my mom laughing in that loud way, I knew it had to be Uncle Wood. When I walked into the kitchen, she was dancing around. Spinning around like she was dancing with the coffee pot. Twirling in a circle before setting it back on the coffee maker.

She skipped over to me and grabbed my face with both of her hands. She kissed both of my cheeks while holding my face. I squirmed away from her, but I liked it.

"Guess who is on his way to see his favorite nephew?" she asked, twirling again.

"How could I ever figure that one out? Seriously, Mom. Settle down!" I shook my head as she held her side. Her crazy kitchen dancing seemed to be catching up with her.

But she didn't slow down. She just held her side in that funny way and kept it up. "How great is that?" she sang. I kept my face blank. My uncle is cool. And it was awesome that she was happy. But we already had plans today.

"*So* great," I said and forced a smile. Then I added like I'd just remembered, "Can J and Flint still come over to hang out and watch fireworks?" We'd planned to celebrate my birthday today, but nothing too fancy.

"I think that sounds perfect. In fact, maybe I should see if their families want to come. Wood is always hoping to catch up with Big Anne," Mom said. Flint's mom is a lot of fun and has a huge personality like Flint. That's really why she's "big," and not just because Flint's older sister is named Annie. I could tell Mom was getting more excited. If that was even possible. "Of course, maybe we should have thought of that before today. Last-minute plans don't always work for everyone. But then again," she said, starting to swirl around the kitchen again as she pulled out my Cheerios and a bowl, "sometimes unexpected plans are the very best kind."

CHAPTER 4
SAY UNCLE

"Sugar!" I heard Uncle Wood holler as he stepped inside and my mom flew into his arms. "Hey, how ya doin'? There's my baby sistah!"

He pulled away for a moment to look at her. She was a little breathless. His eyes traveled down to her hands clutching below her ribs and lingered there for just a moment. But then my mom leaned over to help him with his luggage and packages, and his attention turned to that.

"Come in, come in," Mom said. "How was the flight? May I get you something to drink?"

"Why yes you may, May-Ree," Uncle Wood said, drawing out her name and making his accent even stronger than usual. "I'll have a vodka. With vodka and vodka!" and busted out laughing with my mom.

This is one of their typical exchanges. It has something to do with my grandmother, but I never really got the whole story there. They don't really get into joking about drinking with me around. In fact, Mom suddenly seemed to remember that point and started shushing him. Uncle Wood straightened up and put a really exaggerated serious expression on his face. But then he looked up and saw me standing behind Mom, and his smile got big again.

"Good *Lawd,* babe, what in the world are you feeding this child?" he bellowed. "Albert Christian, you've grown half a foot since I last saw you! My head'll explode if I have to look up to talk to my nephew! Of course, that situation is inevitable since it appears I'm shrinking with each passing day." He sighed and rolled his eyes.

My mom giggled.

"Hi, Uncle Wood," I said, blushing a little. It always felt funny when people talked about how I looked. Since I'd started middle school and grown four inches last year, that only happens like every time I run into an adult who hasn't seen me in a while. But unlike other people who'd just jabber on and be clueless, he seemed to get it. He's always been really good like that. I think he'd be my favorite uncle even if he weren't my only one. So instead of giving me a big bear hug like he gave my mom, he stepped back and straightened his blazer. His eyes looked soft behind his wire-framed glasses, and he stroked his beard. Then he stuck out his hand to shake mine.

"Well, sorry for the outburst, but you are looking handsome and grown-up as ever, sir," he said. "And as it *should* be ... am I wrong, or does America share her birthday week with someone we know and love?"

"Yes, sir," I said. His Southern accent and classy look always kick-started my best manners. "It's my twelfth birthday on Wednesday."

"Is it *reeeaahly?*" he drawled. "Well, thank *Gawd*. Because if it wasn't, I'd feel really silly for bringing *this*!"

And just then I noticed an odd-shaped suitcase. Really, it looked like a funny duffle bag, except it was made from hard plastic. I remembered that Uncle Wood had a lot of weird packing stuff from when he had to transport art to shows or buyers. But whatever was in this particular strange bag, it was clearly for me.

"Can I open it now?" I asked.

My mom smiled and said, "Sure, sweetie. Fine with me."

"Well, of course. Open it, man! I think you're gonna love this. Go for it, Albert."

I flipped the outside latches and popped the top of the case open. I had to unzip a lining inside. Then I pulled out a long rectangular shape that was heavy and covered with several layers of bubble wrap. I pulled at the strong, clear tape until it started to unravel. Finally, the bubble fell away, and I couldn't believe it. There was a brand-new Zero skateboard underneath all of the wrap. The wheels started spinning a little as I pulled it out. I had been stalking this skateboard relentlessly.

"Oh man!" I said. "Thank you, Uncle Wood! This is awesome! I can't believe it."

Uncle Wood smiled. "I'm so glad you like it. But that's not even the best part. Turn it over."

I flipped the board over expecting a really good design on the deck. Most boards have really wild pictures— some are known for their style or color. Some can be over the top and would not be allowed in my house. But most are really interesting. Uncle Wood probably picked out a really cool one for me.

When I flipped it over, I was shocked. Even my mom let out a gasp. The board was filled with the brightest greens and reds and yellows, a bizarre, beautiful scene. And right in the middle of it, stretching all the way to the bright blue sky, was a crazy-cool Oris Hart tree.

"No way!" I held it up and looked at it. I couldn't take my eyes off it. "It's so awesome! Is it real?"

"If by 'real' you mean that Oris's brush touched this very piece of wood, it is absolutely real. But he just did the tree. The rest of the background was on the board, and he painted over it."

"Oh wow. I don't … I … just, wow. This is amazing!" I didn't know what to say. I felt like my body was made of electricity. I held the board and looked at the tree. It was white and round and glowing. I almost felt like I might start to cry. Which was crazy for a kid who was turning twelve years old!

I couldn't believe my uncle would do something like that for me. Or that the incredible Oris Hart would. Now I'd have a piece of art with me as I boarded, a picture made just for me that reminded me of my dad. It made me feel really pumped. I couldn't wait to get outside. I thought about Flint swearing that a new tricked-out pair of cleats took a full minute off his fastest time running the mile at football practice. At the very least, this board was connected to my family and to my favorite artist. Two things that are pretty awesome all by themselves.

Mom laughed looking at my face and said, "Go on, birthday boy," and gave me a kiss on the cheek.

I hugged Uncle Wood hard and fast, then grabbed my helmet off the bench and jogged out the back door.

I made my way over toward Mission Dolores, listening to the soft whirring of my wheels like I was streaming my favorite music. I cut through a side alley near the high school and saw the familiar bright graffiti that glowed across the plain cinderblock. It looked fierce to me—it made the boring concrete look alive. A second, shorter wall in front separated a small row of flowers and plants from the sidewalk and narrowed to only a few inches wide. I pushed hard with my foot to get some speed on the flat surface, then busted up to slide down its length. I landed perfectly and whipped around, popping my new board up once I'd stopped. The air was starting to feel wet and cool. The fog was going to settle in thick soon. Even as my skin began to prickle with the dripping breeze, I hardly noticed I'd forgotten my hoodie.

I thought Flint must be onto something, about the force of special things. It felt like I almost had a kind of superpower with my Oris tree with me. What an amazing way to start my birthday.

It made me think that the next year was going to be the best yet.

CHAPTER 5
SICK

Since we're about to go back to school, here's a pop quiz.

Question: When is a pulled muscle not a pulled muscle?

Answer: When it is cancer.

Now I feel really dumb that even though I've watched my mom hold her side funny so many times, I didn't say *Hey, maybe go to the doctor for that.* Or, *Don't you think it's weird that you pulled your muscle and you can't remember how you did it?* Or, *How long does it take for a pulled muscle to heal, anyway?* I feel like there are lots of things I should've said. I feel bad that even though it's a given that Mom looks after me, there's no one but me to look after my mom.

But finally, after Uncle Wood had come to visit and see me for my birthday, he said something about it.

"Lord, babe, what in the world did you do? That side-grabbing is starting to look like a nervous twitch ... or a signature dance move."

My mom smiled. "You know my signature dance move is this!" She started to dance around the house.

As she rocked around on her feet, my uncle started singing that Drifters song, "Save the Last Dance for Me." I laughed, remembering the first time I'd heard them talk about "beach music"—the songs with the shuffling dances people did where Mom and Uncle Wood had grown up. When I was really little, I'd heard them use that expression, and I thought it meant we were going to the beach. Even though it was nighttime and we were at home. I cried when I'd found out we weren't actually going to the beach, and then I cried harder when they laughed at me. But now it made me smile.

Even with the happy memory, the beach music dance party normally would not have been very cool, since Flint and J had come over to hang out at the house. But Flint started whooping it up when he heard the song. I'm guessing Big Anne likes beach music too. He jumped down off the counter and took my mom's hand and tried to dance with her. Which was a mess and hilarious.

By the end, even though we didn't really know the song, we all hollered, "Save the last dance for me!" It was pretty sweet. And for sure a summer special occasion. No way would you ever catch me busting out a song like that at school. When we stopped, my mom was smiling and panting a little bit. And holding her side.

Uncle Wood looked at it in a hard way. "Seriously, sissy, get someone to look at that."

"Got it," Mom said, and when Uncle Wood raised his eyebrows, she said, "Okay! Okay!"

She went over to her laptop and punched a few keys. "It looks like I can get in with the TargetCare nurse at the college next week. If it ends up being a thing, she can get me in to my doctor."

"Perfecto!" Uncle Wood said. "Just want you to take care of yourself, girl. You ain't as young as you used to be."

"Dang!" Flint said, and Jabari started laughing.

"And yet I am oh, so much younger than you, big brother," Mom said.

"Touché, my dear," Uncle Wood laughed.

So not only did I not tell my mom to see the doctor, I forgot when she had the appointment. This is what I'm saying. I really dropped the ball.

The day she'd gone to the TargetCare nurse at the college, I was over at Flint's trying to make a ramp in his backyard.

We were hoping to add some videos to our YouTube channel devoted to skateboarding. We probably had a couple hundred views on two of our videos—one of Flint catching a football while cruising on a bowl and the one of my pool-noodle goof. We thought if we really spent some time on our channel, we could maybe get a real following. Then maybe get sponsored.

So, the whole time my mom was at the nurse, then the doctor, then calling Big Anne who went to be with her while they run some crazy tests, I was clueless and building stuff and planning with Flint about skateboarding videos.

Until finally Mr. Peterson came home. It was weird for him to be there in the afternoon. He works at

Wells Fargo, not as a bank teller but as someone who helps businesses get money. Like, he helps movie studios get the money they need to make big-time movies. He usually comes home around dinnertime but then has to work some at night. Sometimes he goes back into the office once Flint is in bed. Sometimes he has to be on a conference call at the house, and we have to stay really quiet. There was a time when I'd paid a lot of attention to what dads did and how they were around or gone, and I noticed a lot about Mr. Peterson because I like him a lot, and I noticed a lot about Jabari's dad, too, because he creates amazing things.

But at the time, I didn't clue in to how weird it was for him to be home. Or for him to stand at the doorway and watch us. Or for him to be so quiet instead of whooping it up like Flint does. They are usually very much the same that way.

And maybe I would have gone forever without noticing it, but finally Flint said something.

"Hey, Pops, what's the deal? You wanna try to jump this baby?"

We'd set up some packing crates with plywood on top that we had found behind Blackhawk Hardware. It sort of had the shape of a ramp, though it looked pretty shaky.

Mr. Peterson smiled, but something wasn't right with his eyes. Have you ever seen someone smile, but instead of making them look happy, the smiling made them look sad? I had never seen a sad smile before. Mr. Peterson was sad smiling, and he did not answer Flint. He was looking at me.

"Guys, we need to talk for a minute," he said. "Can y'all finish up and come on inside?"

Flint looked at me with his eyebrows raised. I wondered if we were in trouble for taking the stuff from Blackhawk, even though it had been propped up against the dumpster. My mind started racing with what I was going to say. Maybe we could tell him the Blackhawk guys had asked us to take it away.

Flint must have had the same thought because he muttered under his breath, "Uh oh. Bobo?"

I've seen Mr. Peterson before when Flint had been in trouble, and he's usually pretty loud and mad. I didn't think this was a Juan Bobo situation. When Mr. Peterson had been called out of work by Father Russo after we wrote our names and SKATEBOARDING RULES in the wet cement on the newly fixed sidewalk in front of Holy Hands Catholic School, he had gone nuts. When the realization that we had messed up sunk in, we'd tried to run and hide. Which had not worked out so well for us … with our names drying in the concrete.

"God Aw*mighty*!" Mr. Peterson had hollered, shaking his head. "Geniuses!"

It was something we could laugh about later.

This seemed very different.

So even though we weren't nearly done, we both decided we should go on inside. And Mr. Peterson sat down and started talking. I was so focused on what we were in trouble for that it took me a minute to realize he wasn't upset with us. But it was way, way worse than that. Because he was talking about my mom and saying she was at the hospital.

I heard him, but I sort of didn't hear him. A bunch of his words started bumping together. "Tests," "doctors," "unsure." And then one that made a shiver run up my back. "Surgery."

"You all right, Albert?"

Mr. Peterson stopped talking and put a hand on my arm.

I was embarrassed at how he was looking at me so close in my face, but I was glad he was holding on to me. I felt really shaky, and his hand was strong and warm. All of a sudden, I thought of my own dad. And then my mom. I felt like I was going to be sick.

But I didn't say anything about that.

"I'm fine."

How many times have I told this lie? It should have been easy. I tried to say it strong, but it came out weird. I looked at the ground.

"I want to see my mom."

"Of course you do," Mr. Peterson said, but his voice was strange too.

It was like he was saying one thing but trying to figure out how to say something else. He bit his lip, and then he cleared his throat.

"The thing is, she's at the hospital right now, with the very best doctors, folks who can take really good care of her. And Big Anne is there. I know she wants to see you as soon as she's able, but right now we need to sit tight. As soon as we know the plan, I'll take you up there. I promise."

His hand squeezed my arm a little bit, kind of urgently. "Albert? I'll tell you what all's going on, Okay?

I know this is really hard and unexpected. But you're going to be just fine."

I nodded and tried to smile, and then the tears came. It was like his sad smile was contagious and had infected my face. I feel so many things, and I've worked hard to keep them down, but for the first time I wasn't sure if this was the kind of feeling that I should shut off. It wasn't like being mad. It did feel like it was too much, though, out of control. I closed my eyes and thought of a huge crashing wave and then the calm hiss on the sand as it spreads itself thin over smooth shells and rocks that are slick. I let the wave of my feelings go with that surf, and I felt calm again.

I was fine when we went back to the house to get my things to stay at the Petersons for a while. And I was fine when I ate a few bites of dinner. I was even fine when Big Anne tucked me into Flint's trundle bed and gave me a hug that was strong and sweet, just like she is. I was fine for all of those times.

I was doing okay until Flint told me goodnight and shut the lights out in the room and I stared at the ceiling. I couldn't sleep. I played through the crazy day like scenes in a movie, the first half on fast-forward, the second half in slow-mo. I replayed it again and again, and all of a sudden, I was not fine at all. It felt like a block of concrete had dropped onto my chest when I remembered first talking to Mr. Peterson. And what he had said at the end. Or what I thought I had heard him say.

I wanted to remember that he had said my mom would be just fine. But that's not what it was.

He had said that *I* would be okay.

FALL

CHAPTER 6
THE MORE THINGS CHANGE

There's a picture on Mom's desk of me when I was little, wearing a pair of red cowboy boots that I really loved. I wore them everywhere I went, even to bed sometimes. But after trucking through the creek by the park in them one afternoon, they changed. Even though Mom had dried them in the sun the next day and they looked pretty good, they started coming apart at the bottom. And they felt weird from the inside. They were just pretty messed up where you couldn't see, all cracked and crumbling around the edges.

When I looked in the mirror today, nothing had changed. You wouldn't guess how bad it felt on the inside. And I knew it was more important than ever to be solid. I was trying hard to act like everything was normal.

But there's nothing normal about being in the hospital. There's nothing normal about your mom trying to act cheery when you finally see her. She'd looked weird and small in the metal bed, and everything was cold and sad in her ugly gray room. There's nothing normal about being sick, and there's nothing normal about having a surgery that takes out a bunch of your insides and keeps you in the hospital for two weeks.

Finally when Mom had come home, it was time to get ready to go back to school. I've never liked when things aren't really clear, and this year was the worst. I didn't like not knowing who would take me to school or if I'd need to take the bus. Or whether I'd have art class or if it was full and I'd have to take drama or chorus instead. There's a lot of stress with not knowing what to expect. And Holy Hands has a crazy policy where we don't get our schedule until the first day, so no one has time to complain or try to change anything. (Maybe it's the parents who are crazy, actually). All we get beforehand is our advisor and our locker assignment and the date for our orientation meeting.

When we go for orientation, we set up our lockers and do a bunch of paperwork. Our teachers aren't even there. It's a way to ease in, I guess. Usually that's the one part I like because Mom and I would go for smoothies after, and we'd talk about how painful school can be but how it's also nice to have a fresh start.

My start is not feeling very fresh so far. No Mom and no smoothies this year. Big Anne picked me up with Flint and J already in the car. I was glad to see them, but it was kind of strange too. No one cracked any jokes. It was like we were at the library or something. Or like we were with Mom and she needed to rest. I think we were afraid of slipping up and busting ourselves if we started talking too much, so we just kept our mouths shut. Which was probably smart. But it felt bad.

So I just looked out of the car windows the entire way to Holy Hands. There were posters stapled to the telephone poles about a parade for 9/11. My stomach started to hurt. The last time I went to school, my mom had been completely fine. I just kept wishing that things were like they'd been before.

And then my wish came true, but in the worst possible way. Because right after we signed in and got our supply list and checked into the gym to pick up our new gym shorts and mouth guards, I turned the corner to head to my locker, and I heard the unmistakable voice of Pat McBee—and it was just as obnoxious as ever.

He was messing with Dori Martin, but I didn't know why at first. Then she turned her face to the side, and I could tell that she'd gotten glasses over the summer. Right away I could see that her eyes were red and puffed up, and it had to be from crying and not from the drops they sometimes put in people's eyes at the appointment. Dori is a pretty tiny person, but somehow her glasses were totally huge. They seemed to take up half her face and kept sliding down her nose. I don't know why she would've decided on that look, but maybe someone else had picked them for her. Or she had gotten them and then wanted to change, but it had been too late. Maybe the money had been spent, and she had to live with her choice. Like when I'd gotten those new wheels that seemed so great at Mission Skate, and then they looked completely dumb the second I had them on my board, even though I'd been obsessed with them for weeks and buying them had taken a bunch of my allowance.

When Pat saw her, he laughed out loud. Like, forced loud laughs that make everyone turn around in the hall. Laughs that are so showy and noisy they make you want to cover your ears. He was fake-laughing so hard and so loud that he dropped this big notebook that was supposed to be in his locker with the rest of his school supplies, and all his papers started falling out. It made a huge mess where everyone was trying to walk by.

As if that wasn't enough of a commotion, he pointed right at Dori and started hollering, "Oh my *God*. Someone let Gollum into the school! *My precious my precious my precious!*"

He doubled over, cracking himself up. And it was really ugly and really mean and really too bad—because the second he said "Gollum," it was like hitting a target with a dart right in the center of the circle. She *did* look like a nice Gollum. Last year, no way. But this year, with those huge glasses and her hair slicked back in her ponytail and her super sad expression ... bull's-eye.

When that happened, Dori just looked at me with this pleading kind of expression. I glared at Pat and started to feel myself getting really mad. I tried to think of my strategies, but my mind was blank. I could feel my brain racing to land on something that would make me calm, but nothing was coming. And the longer nothing came, the madder I felt.

"What's the matter, Mama's boy? You gonna cry?" Pat said in his ugliest voice.

And after that, I just lost it. My mind didn't even care about strategies as I kicked his notebook on the floor so hard that it crashed into the lockers across the hall with a loud smack. Pat shoved Dori out of the way and started to come toward me. I felt my hands ball into fists.

Just then Flint appeared from out of nowhere. He stood on the other side of Dori and put his head to the side.

"Hey, well, no worries, Jabba—clearly the school is open to all kinds."

The kids around us laughed at the reference to the gross *Star Wars* blob, and by the expression on Pat's face, it got to him. He looked pretty mad. But I could tell that the laughter had changed the scene. I started to unclench my hands. Had I really planned to hit somebody? Even if it was Pat, and even if he deserved it, that was a terrible idea. What would Mom do if I got in trouble for fighting? What was wrong with me?

Pat looked at us for a moment, and then he shook his head and walked past us. He bumped into Flint as he went by, "accidentally" knocking him on the shoulder. Flint grabbed his side in an exaggerated way and made a funny face. Jabari jogged up to us and looked back and forth with a confused expression.

"What happened? Don't tell me he's started in already?"

We nodded, and Jabari rolled his eyes. "No way. Did Albie have to play peacemaker before school even officially starts?"

Flint gave me a quick glance. I looked at the floor. To his credit, Flint didn't correct J. I could usually let a NWLWL rip without a problem at all. But at that moment, the lie hung in the air like something rotten.

CHAPTER 7
BIG SISTER

On the ride home, everyone was quiet again. I was feeling worse by the minute. But then Big Anne pulled up to the house, and I saw several cars out front. This is not unusual these days. It means that someone is over, helping Mom. I could feel my mood get better when I saw those cars.

From the very beginning, once folks had heard about what was going on with Mom, friends and neighbors were everywhere I turned. This was very cool. It made me feel really good. Kind of the opposite of how I felt at orientation. As I walked toward the door, I thought back to how many helpers had appeared since we found out about the cancer.

First came the women—Big Anne, Dr. Pahlavi, Mrs. Martin, and all of my friends' moms from the middle school. All of the teachers, even ones from my preschool, so many I had not seen for years. And lots of folks from church. The women's circles, taking turns to come to pray the rosary with Mom. The knitting club with a pretty prayer shawl. The youth group leaders.

And with the women came food, more than we could fit in our fridge. Old Mrs. Estes next door offered hers for the parts that would not fit. Mrs. Flynn, whose son owns the sub shop on the corner, even gave us part of his huge meat freezer to help store the extras. Big Anne showed me how to thaw things out and how to use the oven for each one.

Mom and I laughed at all of this food. We'd never eaten so well. Mom wasn't what you'd call a "foodie." Our meals had usually been pretty simple. I didn't know if I was a foodie or not, but after tasting all that great stuff, I decided I just might be.

After the women came Father Russo. He said special prayers with us, and that was pretty cool but a little weird, only because I was used to seeing him at Mass instead of sitting on my couch, right next to my kneepads and helmet and a muddy T-shirt I'd forgotten to put in the laundry. He glanced at it really quick but kept his face still. In some jobs people have to keep their faces from showing anything. It's pretty wild. I wondered what my face looked like when I was trying to stay solid. Probably not as straight as Father Russo's.

Then came Sister, which is what Mom and I call her. But she's really Ms. Margaret Fields to everyone else. Not everyone knows that she used to be a nun. Most people just know her as a middle school teacher. The only good thing in my school year so far was knowing that I would have her as my advisor this year.

It'd been a while since she'd come to our house, but when I saw Sister, she was just as I remembered. She's a short person with light hair and big blue eyes, but she takes up a lot of space. Kind of like a cyclone—a funny, nice cyclone.

I heard her before I saw her. She was yelling about something with my mom, and when I walked in, I saw that my mom was crying—because she was laughing so hard. I never heard the joke though; as soon as I entered the room, Sister raced over and threw her arms around me. These days most people don't know whether they should hug me or not, but she didn't hesitate. She never does. That's one of the best things about her.

"Kid!" she hollered, holding me back and looking at me. "How're you doing, buddy?" She held onto me and looked right into my eyes with her big blue ones. "I know this is rough. But your mom looks great. How're you holding up?"

"I'm fine," I said and looked at my happy mom. I was actually telling the truth at that moment.

"Excellent! Well, if you weren't, that would be okay, too. I mean that. You need to do you. Whatever it is. Feel the feelings, even the hard ones. They always make themselves known in some kind of way."

She let go of me and turned back to my mom. "So, what's the schedule here, Mary? I know you've started chemo."

"Yes. That was … difficult. But they figured out how to manipulate the medicine so it isn't as hard to tolerate. I'll be having treatments once a month for six months. Each treatment will be administered over twenty-four hours, instead of over five. They'll do it at the hospital in case there're any problems."

I looked at Sister quickly. The chemo had been a disaster at first, bad enough that they wouldn't let me see Mom until they figured it out. Or, at least, that had been the plan.

The thing was, I really couldn't *not* see her. Mom wasn't supposed to have been in the hospital at all when she'd started chemo. But her treatment had made her sick when it was supposed to fight the cancer and make her well. I was so glad that J's mom had been staying with us during this time and she had known what to do when it got to be too much. Still, it had meant Mom had to go back to the hospital she'd just gotten out of. It made me crazy. I just had to go visit her and know for myself that she was okay.

And that had been something Jabari and Flint had both understood. They agreed they'd want the same thing. So they came up with a plan to help me see my mom.

Flint had Uber on his phone—strictly for emergencies—but if this hadn't been an emergency, what in the world was? His account had been set up by his sister, Annie, before she'd left for college, and she'd accidentally had the email receipt go to her. His parents meant to change it but had forgotten to do it. Flint had said he'd handle his sister. And he said to leave the talking to him when we got in the car, and that was fine with me.

Since Jabari's mom works at the hospital, she had a name tag that could get us inside. We'd listened in while she'd been talking to Big Anne on the phone about Mom and got the scoop on where she was. We were having to sneak around, and that wasn't usually cool with Jabari. It had meant a lot to me that he would put that to the side. Flint stole the old name tag out of the car keys bowl in case we needed it to open the doors.

When we got there, we didn't even have to check in at the front desk. We just walked past it to the elevators and pressed the "five" button. We got off and tried to look like we knew what we were doing. When a nurse started to come over to us, Flint launched our distraction plan and backed into a tall cart with a bunch of food trays and knocked them over. Jabari rushed around to pick up the stuff as the nurse ran toward us. They both gave me a look, and I knew it was my chance.

I ducked behind the cart and then backed down the hall, crouched over bent in half, while Flint made excuses and a bigger mess on the other side. I glanced up at the room numbers and saw I just had to go around the corner to get to Mom. I straightened up and started to move very quickly. Her door was in sight—but then I heard the worst sound ever.

From behind her closed door, I could hear her crying. And a low murmuring of voices. And then crying again. Not the kind of soft crying like when we'd watched *The Pursuit of Happyness* together, with silent tears streaming down her face. This was a sound I had not ever heard before, not one that I could remember. My mom was sobbing.

I stood completely still, my heart pounding. Just a few more steps and I would be at her door, inside of it. But I could not move. I almost couldn't breathe.

Then, as sure as I'd wanted to see my mom, I didn't want to see her. What had I thought I was going to do? Was she sad or scared? Was the chemo hurting her again? What was I going to say?

I turned around and walked back to the scene of the crime. Most of the mess had already been picked up. The nurse was not happy. She was looking at Flint. "But that makes no sense. Okay, tell me again what you boys are doing up here?"

Flint and J looked at me. I shook my head just slightly and then cleared my throat. The nurse jumped a little at the noise and looked startled when she turned and saw there were actually three of us.

"Just leaving, sorry, wrong floor! We're here to see my mom. She works here." Like usual, the words came out of my mouth super easy.

Jabari's mouth fell open, but he quickly shut it.

"Thanks for all of your help. Bye!" I said.

We booked it out of there ASAP.

I'd felt bad that we could have all gotten into trouble and that I hadn't even seen my mom. But the guys understood. Or, at least, they made me feel like everything was all right. When I told them I just couldn't do it, they nodded. I was ready to say that the door was locked or that another nurse was blocking me, but they didn't ask me. When I thought about the crying, it made me feel sick. I didn't want to talk about it.

So when Sister mentioned chemo, I could feel my face getting really hot. I tried to stay cool. There was something about not being honest with Sister that felt really crappy. What was my problem? It's not like Sister or Mom or anyone else even knew what we had tried to do. Still, I was starting to sweat. But she wasn't even looking at me. She was peering into Mom's face. She reached over and held her hands.

"I heard that it was bad, and I'm really sorry. Thank God they were able to adjust it for you. I mean, honestly. What the heck—is it really going to be the *medicine* that makes you feel miserable?" She shook her head and smiled at Mom and squeezed her hand. Then she turned to me.

"So, Albert, I think we have some good news, but I'll let you be the judge of that."

"Okay."

"Not only are you in my advisory this year, you're also in my English and science classes. So that's a lot of Fields Time! But I think you can handle it. And hey, listen, we're going to be putting together some cool stuff to send for Pope Francis's visit to New York, so I'll definitely need your artistic expertise."

"Oh wow. Yeah, of course," I said.

"And I was just talking to your mom about scheduling some time to just check in. Just for you to have a place to talk about what's going on. If that seems all right to you."

I don't know if she could see the relief on my face, but I was definitely feeling it. Sister is someone who has my back. Not that I'm the only one who feels that way about her. She's legendary at my school. She's in charge of all the student assemblies for Holy Hands, and at every one she would end with teaching us something in a cool way. Once it was about the Renaissance and how to be a Renaissance man or Renaissance woman in life. Once it was about poems—she read three, and I didn't get bored even once. I still remember them: "Do not go gentle into that good night" and "Sonnet 29" and "Sam."

Even though I haven't had a class with her yet, I've heard about her first-day performances. By the end of the first class, she had everyone pumped up and excited. But behaving too. Sister doesn't mess around.

And she's wicked smart. I know the first thing she does at the beginning of each school year is have everyone in her class fill out a notecard with their names, favorite movie or book, and their contact info. Then she picks up all the cards in order and flips through them one time. She looks at each card for maybe a couple seconds before she sets them down. And then, without peeking at them at all, she goes through the entire list, naming every kid in order and saying something about their favorites. She gets every name right. She knows every movie and every book.

It sets a tone.

Some kids don't know what to make of Sister, and I understand that. She's a force, and people like that can be scary. But once you see that force in action to help you, then you know that her big personality is a good thing. When times get rough, that's what you want backing you up. Like when you don't understand an assignment and feel stupid and want to give up. Or when Pat decides you're the number-one humiliation target of the week, and you need a teacher to get what's happening and to know what to do.

Or when you're a little kid and pissed off because your dad is gone. And you fight for no reason that makes sense at the time except for the best and worst reason ever. Which everyone knows, even if they act like they don't remember. And you can't say that you're scared and worried. Because you're four and you don't have the right words.

So instead you tug at your socks, rip them from your feet, throw them against the wall, and scream that they are burning you. You won't put them back on because they hurt too bad. When I screamed and threw my socks, and then my shoes, I felt a little bit better. Even though I'd known what I was saying didn't make sense, I didn't care. I didn't care I was making everyone nervous. Right after my dad had died, I didn't care about anything.

The grown-ups hadn't known what to do. They said to my already-wrecked mom that maybe Holy Hands wasn't the right place for me. Maybe my tantrums would scare other children. Maybe I needed to go to a special school where shoes and socks and rules weren't so important.

That's when you want someone marching—I mean, marching like a freaking Storm Trooper—right up to people and getting in their faces. And closing the door not like a slam but still hard and quick. And talking and talking while you wait on the other side hearing the words rise through the wall like a punk rock song. And when the door opens again, to march back up to you.

And look you in your face with eyes so blue and big and say, "I know it hurts. If those socks and shoes hurt, you don't have to wear them."

As soon as I'd heard those words and looked into Sister's eyes, I did the thing that I should have done before. I started to cry. I cried and cried while she held me. Her arms had been like a life jacket, firm and tight. The other adults stood around us until they were tired or bored or had somewhere else to be. But she hadn't acted like there was anywhere else she had to go. She held onto me for as long as it took, rocking me on the floor of the classroom that would still be my classroom, until all of my tears were gone.

CHAPTER 8
HOME WORK

———

ands End is my very favorite place. And not just because it's really pretty, right beside the massive water with cool trees and flowers along the trails. A lot of California is pretty. A lot of San Francisco is pretty, even for a city. I've been to New York and Chicago and Charleston with Mom and Uncle Wood, so I know a little bit about that. But Lands End is not just nice to look at. I like it because I love to hike the trails there with Flint and Jabari. Unlike skateboarding, that's not something we get to do very often.

Whenever tourists come to San Francisco, they all want to go there. Today a big bunch of them on Segways came busting past Flint and J and me on the trail. It was completely nuts.

"Whoa!" Flint hollered as the scooters came cruising beside him. "Way to get back to nature!" He cracked himself up.

Jabari looked embarrassed and tried to shush him, but that just got him going more.

"Naw, that's okay, I get it," Flint yelled. "It would be in-san-a-*tee* to walk a trail through the woods when you can do it on a motorized scooter. I totally get it! This is why America is number one in the world for physical fitness."

Flint has started to sound a lot like his mom, who has a really sarcastic sense of humor. Sometimes she says things, and you think, man, she's crazy, but then you realize she's just messing with you. Big Anne always makes people laugh. And she has always been really cool about taking us to the hiking trails at Lands End whenever she meets with her book club at the Cliff House.

"Yeah, but is a scooter really any different than a skateboard?" Jabari asked. He always sees every side to every issue. Which is pretty cool unless he is seeing something the opposite of you.

"Is it different? Seriously, Bambi? I think that hair gel has seeped into your brain. Are you suffering from sunstroke? Do you need to lie down? Do not evah, *evah* question the superior athletic skill required to maneuver a skateboard!"

When he really gets going, Flint's Southern accent comes out awfully thick. And he was in top form now. "It is night and day to a *Segway*."

Flint said that last word in a voice that sounded like he was holding his nose.

"Well, I thought maybe you'd prefer a Segway after all that book report homework," Jabari snickered.

Flint apparently had not heard of Sister's amazing first-day notecard tradition. As a joke he'd written down that his favorite book was a random one sitting on the shelf across from his desk, *The Companion to the Catechism of the Catholic Church*. It wasn't so funny once we were assigned a report on our favorites and Flint's choice was over nine hundred pages long. After begging and pleading, he had worked out a deal with Ms. Fields so he didn't have to do all of it, but he still had to write his report on a huge chunk of that book. He had been working nonstop for days.

I agreed that it was silly that people would Segway in a place where it was so pretty to hike, but it didn't offend me. It just seemed like a pretty manic way to experience the coastal trails. The place is one of the coolest I have ever seen. I like to look out over the water. It always makes me feel relaxed. I've been trying to get that feeling as much as I could these days.

When Mom had finished her second round of chemo, we had a big talk. Mom said Dr. Pahlavi met with her at the hospital to learn about meditation and breathing and dealing with pain. She said it was a lot like my strategies I used to control my temper and to stay solid. Mom said she thought I could teach her a lot about all of that.

This idea didn't sound all that great to me. I don't really know how I do my strategies. Just thinking about explaining them made my head hurt. I just didn't want to think about the cancer.

I feel okay when I pretend like it's not happening to us. But cancer is an annoying fire alarm, screeching out that you are about to be in trouble if you don't get your act together. It messes up the simplest things.

Like the things Mom and I could do to have fun together changed. It used to be that we would go for a jog in Golden Gate or take the cable car to Ghirardelli's for hot chocolate. We used to love to play tennis on Saturdays at Dolores Park. When we were missing my dad and we wanted to do something special, we would ride bikes across the bridge to Sausalito and catch the shuttle over to hike in Muir Woods. Not anymore.

But Mom had started to get good at turning boring things into something interesting. Like studying for my vocab test earlier today. I'm actually pretty good at spelling, so it wasn't too painful. But then when Mom was quizzing me, she turned it into a game. After one of my words was *vogue* (I got it right) she said, "Strike a pose."

"What?"

"You know, Madonna."

"Sorry, no."

Her mouth dropped open. I laughed.

"Yeah, I have no idea what you're talking about."

"Well, this is a pop-culture emergency," she said in an exaggerated way and reached across the table for her laptop. She popped it open and punched a few keys. She flipped it around for me to see the video of the singer who I didn't really know, but I saw from YouTube that her name was Madonna. Some crazy-looking dudes danced to her song. Which I got was called "Vogue."

"Cool," I said.

"Very cool," she said. After that, every time I got ten words right, we looked up another Madonna video. That lady has made a lot of music. I liked most of it. "Like a Prayer" and "Frozen" were my favorites. Mom got real quiet watching that last one. When the black shawl hit the ground and broke into a bunch of birds flying away, she got really still. And then she just started to bawl. The tears streaked down her cheeks, just a little at first, then her whole face crumpled. I could feel a lump in my throat. I thought if I swallowed I would cry too. I got this really strong feeling that I could not let it happen. It came over my body so hard—if the tears spilled over, I would explode into a thousand pieces like Madonna's black birds and catch on fire and rain ashes from the sky. I closed my eyes so I couldn't see Mom. I thought of the birds flying, with their wings flapping harder and harder until all that was left were small black dots. As they began to disappear, I felt okay again.

Mom put her hands under her eyes and wiped her face, hard. She took a deep breath and turned back to the computer. I saw her pull my word list back up. Yes. Please. I had never been so happy to see homework in my life.

She started calling out the next row, like nothing had just happened. We kept at the list like that, and when I got the next ten right, the video she picked was strong and fun. Madonna belted out "Express Yourself," and a bunch of muscly dudes worked in some factory where it rained on the inside. There was also a black cat. And then Madonna pretending to be a cat. No worries about getting weepy with that one.

When Flint called to see if I wanted to go with them to Lands End, I had just aced all of my spelling words. Mom was tired but seemed happy. It was perfect, which was not a given these days. On bad days I felt guilty every time I left Mom. Even with the meltdown, this was not a bad day.

CHAPTER 9

RESCUED

"Ten-minute rule," she called when we heard the car honk in the driveway.

I pulled my phone out and waved it to her. "Got it," I said.

She can always count on me to answer her quick if she calls or texts me.

Big Anne was on speakerphone when I got into the car and was talking a million miles a minute. Something her editor did to her last column.

"Right! No, I get it, darlin'. But do you see why you don't want to make the punch line of the joke the headline? Do you see how that completely ruins the whole thing?" Big Anne was using her biggest voice.

Flint rolled his eyes. We looked out the windows at the huge houses while she raged all the way to our drop-off. As she screeched away down El Camino del Mar to meet her book club at the Cliff House, we started walking on the path.

After the Segway tour crashed passed us, the scene was quiet. The path wound around and the massive water appeared on our right. Cool trees twisted in funky designs all around us. I took out my phone and snapped a few pictures so I could draw them later. I was feeling so pumped to be hanging out with the guys—until Jabari asked about my mom. Lots of people ask about her these days, but I could feel Jabari's big eyes looking hard at me when he asked. I squirmed and mumbled the usual.

"Okay, but what is 'fine'? Is the chemo making her feel sick?"

I noticed Flint had stopped tossing his football in the air and was watching me.

The sound of my mom puking in the toilet. The way she fell asleep even when it was the middle of the day and I was talking to her. The picture of her face crumpling. The hard way she wiped her tears. For just a second, I wanted them to know.

But more than that, I wanted to get out from the laser beams of Jabari's stare.

"She has special medicine that makes her feel good instead of sick," I said evenly. "It's a brand-new drug. So, it's totally fine."

"Nice!" Flint said and pitched the ball to J.

Jabari looked at me for just a second longer and then jogged ahead, throwing the ball back. My little white lie worked its magic. Just like they always did.

I caught the ball and faked out J and tossed it behind my back to Flint, who caught it with one hand. Jabari cupped his hands around his mouth like he was a cheering fan. "Gooooo Bo! Bo! Bo!" he chanted.

If Juan Bobo was a nickname for messing up, the abbreviated version was one for classic Flint moves. We'd started calling him Bo once he became obsessed with Bojangles biscuits after visiting family on the East Coast over the summer. He still will not shut up about it.

"Y'all. Seriously. You have not lived until you have partaken of that most-amazing chicken. That beautiful bread. Ahhhh."

"Fast food bread is beautiful?" Jabari wrinkled his nose. "Uh, think I'll pass."

"Bo bread is like tasting heaven on your tongue. It's like Jesus came to earth and wanted to make a most-perfect after-school snack, and it was a Bojangles biscuit. And then he rested. After he ate it. Thank you, Jesus!"

"Easy," I said. I don't particularly love the Jesus talk when it is about being silly. Except I had to agree it really was funny the way Flint said it. And I had tasted Bojangles at Uncle Wood's in Charleston. It was pretty awesome.

"All right, brother. I will cease with the JC talk. And I will remember my sass mouth at confession. And I will offer prayers of thanksgiving for the amazing Bo—"

"Okay, okay!" I laughed.

We kept walking at a pretty good pace. I grabbed a broken stick and used it to pop the ground as I stepped. We were quiet for a minute, except for the crunching of our feet along the path. Suddenly Flint started to turn down toward the Sutro Baths, taking the wide steps a couple at a time, jumping back and forth.

"Yo, Bo, where ya going?" Jabari hollered after him.

"Let's check out the baths," he called back over his shoulder. "Like Abraham Lincoln said, 'Cleanliness is next to godliness.'"

"Ah, sure," Jabari answered flatly, but he followed behind Flint.

The sun was warm on my arms. The sky was a bright blue against the darker water. A light breeze ruffled my thin UNC Tarheels T-shirt. It felt nice and cool against the burning sun.

All of a sudden, we noticed a group of people gathered on the concrete wall close to the bottom. They were huddled together and pointing. Probably tourists, probably someone found a big bunch of birds. That was cool but not a big deal to us. I looked out over the water to see if I could find them.

And that's when I saw it. Out where the surf crashed into the rocks in the shore. At first, I didn't know if it was a rock or a charred piece of wood. Maybe something that had broken off a boat. But then it came into full view.

"Aw, sick! Look at that shark!" Flint said and turned to jump down closer to where the crowd was watching. It was pretty sick in a gross way. I could tell by looking at it that it wasn't a huge animal—just a baby really—but probably as long as my leg from the tip of its nose to the end of its back fin. It had really pretty black and white markings. Somehow it had come in where it was too shallow, and now it was trapped in the surf. As the waves slammed down, it slammed also and rolled over and over, finally hitting the rocks bordering the beach.

With each wave, it was left closer and closer to shore. The tourists started pulling out their phones, snapping pics. One man in a baseball cap started filming.

"Oh man," Jabari said as the last wave left the animal in the shallow water. "This is terrible."

"Let's check it out," Flint said, and we climbed carefully down onto the sand.

I walked up to the shark. It was dark and glistening, with liquid black eyes seeping into its dark skin. The white on its underbelly seemed to glow. It was beautiful.

I squatted down next to it and rubbed my hand across its back to its dorsal. It was as smooth and shiny as thick, wet, black paint.

I looked out into the water. A huge boulder divided the deeper area some yards away from us from the shallow shore. The shark needed to get past the boulder to have any chance to survive.

I stood up and walked around behind it. I kicked my shoes off to the side. Then I reached down and grabbed it from behind its tail fin. I began pulling it back toward the water. It made tracks across the wet sand.

"Al—what're you doin'?" Flint jogged up to me.

I didn't answer him but reached into my pocket and grabbed my phone. I tossed it with one hand, and he caught it. He was shaking his head. I picked up the pace and started to pull harder and faster. I could see Jabari talking to someone near the wall, a girl who was gesturing with her hands. He wasn't watching me.

"Albie! The water is freezing. And that's a shark, friend!"

"A baby shark," I answered over my shoulder, as if that made any real difference. The water began to splash up my leg.

"Yes!" Flint yelled, seeing that I was going in. "A baby *shark*. With a *mother*. Where is *she?* Dude! Seriously. Stop!"

But I kept going. I held on as the waves crashed against my legs and again when the tide going back wanted to pull the big fish from me. When the first wave hit above my waist, I breathed in real fast and held it. Flint was right. The water was so cold. I forced my mind not to think about that. I held on tighter and kept pushing out.

At first, I thought I could just go out to my waist and then let it go. But the current was too strong. If there was any hope of the shark swimming out past the biggest rock, I knew I was going to have to pull it past where the waves were breaking.

As it bobbed along behind me, I could feel the shark try to turn. But as the waves picked up, it seemed to relax. It let me pull him. I wondered if it was possible for it to somehow know that I was trying to help him.

I really was starting to feel cold though. I knew I would have to go fast. I could hear Flint and Jabari yelling to me from the beach, and other people joined in too. I held my breath as a wave broke over my face. I used my free hand to wipe my eyes quickly. They burned. Another wave crashed over me. And then the water was still. I felt the shark tug harder and faster. This was my chance.

I quickly swung around as hard as I could, opened my hand, and then stepped back. For just a tiny second, I wondered if the shark would turn toward me and try to bite me. Or swim back toward the beach, just too tired to fight to swim away. I held my breath again, this time praying that it would take the chance to swim back to where it should have been all along.

It bent back and forth a couple times, and then I saw the white glint of its underbelly flash for just a second. Then it was gone.

My body felt really numb as I turned around, but my heart was beating fast, and I could feel my blood pumping in my ears. I felt strong.

I turned toward the shore and saw Flint and Jabari and a bunch of people on the shore. They started cheering and clapping. A few of them were filming me as I pushed through the current to where I could jog out of the water.

Flint pounded me on the back, and J peeled off his Holy Hands sweatshirt and wrapped it around me. Everyone was really excited and talking at once.

"Man, are you okay?" Jabari asked. I noticed then that I was shaking.

I looked out over the water, and the shark was nowhere in sight. "Yeah," I answered, smiling. "I'm just fine."

CHAPTER 10
FAKE IT UNTIL YOU MAKE IT

Throughout my whole life, people have talked to me about seeing the glass half full. When you're disappointed, it can be hard to think of the things that are good. But it's a strong way to be. Someone smart (but probably not Abraham Lincoln, sorry Flint) once said, "Fake it until you make it." I'm a pro at this. It's kind of crazy how easily stuff comes out of my mouth in bad situations. I just know what to say to fix things. If you do it enough, it becomes sort of a habit. And it trains your brain to focus on the good. On most days when I was in a bad mood and feeling really low, maybe missing my dad, my mind would immediately think, *But I'm really lucky that I have my mom.*

This became a lot harder to do, obviously, when Mom got sick. There were many days when I was really angry about it. One of our first vocab words in language arts this year was *seethe*, and when I learned it, I was so glad for that word. It summed up exactly how I felt. I seethed that my mom was sick when I did not have a dad. I seethed that our family would have to deal with something bad again.

I think because I'd worked so hard with a therapist after my dad died, I never let myself think of screaming or breaking things or beating someone up. Even though that was what I sometimes felt like doing. But since those things were not realistically any of my choices, or in my "toolbox" (speaking of therapists), instead I seethed.

At some point, though, the seething seemed to go away. It just made me too tired to keep it up. Sometimes being angry can make you feel strong. But it's not real. It's a trick. It's like feeling awake because you drank a Coke. Soon it wears off and the feeling goes away, and then you are just more tired. And your problem is still there.

After a while, I wasn't constantly rumbling with anger, but there are still lots of reminders that my mom is sick, like when she has to have her chemo. I'm glad they were able to fix her medicine so it wouldn't hurt her so bad, but it still makes her feel really tired and "blah," as she says. And it makes her look different. Which is sometimes scary and sometimes depressing.

But here's the thing, the glass-half-full thing. Suddenly there were tons of times when the glass didn't seem empty at all. Like when Mom's hair had started to fall out and she decided to go ahead and shave her head. Mom's students knew all about what was going on— because of her diagnosis, she didn't have a bunch of classes this time, but she'd kept her job as advisor to the paper and to the journalism club. And those kids who'd had a bunch of classes and stuff with her were all over it, texting her and writing to her and checking in.

So, my mom texted a picture to her journalism group right after she shaved her head. She was smiling and trying to look happy. She made some kind of joke about not having to worry about bad hair days, but I could see she was shaking when she sent the text. This felt pretty big and pretty strange. Her smooth head was so different than her short blond hair, but her bright pink Burt's Bees lip stuff was so typical. She looked like my mom, and she looked like a complete stranger. I could tell she wanted to cry, but she would not let the tears fall.

That is, until the text replies started dinging on her phone.

She read the first one and squealed as she looked at her phone. Then, *ding*, and she cried out again, her hand coming up to cover her mouth. *Ding, ding, ding,* three more times, and by the end she was full-on sobbing.

"Mom? Mom! What is it? What's wrong?" I rushed over, and she passed me her phone. I saw that all of the text replies were pictures. Each one from a different student. Each one showing a big smile, or a funny expression, or a funky handwritten note—and a bald head. All of the students who texted back to my mom had shaved their heads. There were even two girls.

"Oh man! Oh wow." My mouth dropped open, and I looked at Mom.

She was laughing and crying and looking at the phone and scrolling up and down for me to see, and I was laughing with her. All of a sudden, her phone started belting out "Ave Maria," her ringtone. She answered it and started yammering to Carlos, from picture #2, her voice loud with excitement.

I thought about that and about what people will do to show someone they care. Sometimes it's unsurprising that they care. Like Big Anne or Sister or Flint and J. Sometimes it's unexpected, like Mom's students. And sometimes it's just plain unbelievable.

CHAPTER 11

BONNIE AND CLYDE

After I rescued that shark near Cliff House, a crazy thing happened. *The Chronicle* ran a story on it. They had asked about me and my family, so they learned about Mom ... and about my dad ... and they wrote about all of it. Then News 4 San Francisco ran a story on it, and they showed the video of me crashing through the waves. Mom's mouth literally fell open when her favorite station, CNN, picked it up. And all of a sudden it was all over the internet. Which was sort of weird, but it happened so fast that I didn't have time to really think about how I felt about it.

"Dude!" Flint hollered, as he and Jabari came crashing through my front door the day I was on CNN. "You're taking off on Twitter!"

"I'm not on Twitter," I answered stupidly.

"Uh, I beg to differ, son. You are on everywhere. You're the real-life Shark Kid! Of course, I had to upload your video to my Twitter. But I gave you full credit. For being the awesome hero that you are. I just said I was your bestie. And your swimming coach."

"It *is* pretty cool," Jabari added. "Someone told me they saw your video on YouTube. I think that girl Marissa uploaded it. Or maybe it's the version from CNN. Wait," he paused dramatically, "let me search you online."

"Aw, come on." I was feeling pretty embarrassed at this point. But also a little excited.

"Um, Albie? You're coming up ten different ways! This is crazy!"

Flint started laughing. "You da *man*! Your stardom is seeping all the battery out of my phone, dude. Can I use your charger?"

Already he was walking over to the side table where Mom and I keep our mail and phones. If I had a dollar for every time Flint had busted into my house with his phone at two percent, I'd be a seriously rich man. Perfect timing for a break too. It was starting to get a little weird.

I grabbed my board from under the coat hooks lining the wall by the back door. "Anyone up for a run?"

"Sweet! Oh yes."

I had to hand it to Jabari. He still had a bandage on his knee from last weekend's tricks. He always hesitated before trying something new and fast. Maybe that was his problem, which was what Mom would call a "self-fulfilled prophecy." I think it's because J is so smart, he can't *not* think about consequences. Another of Mom's favorite phrases: "healthy fear."

Sometimes maybe it's smart to be afraid.

We grabbed our stuff, minus Flint's phone on the counter, and headed to the door. My board hit the stools at the island and crashed out of my hand. Jabari winced. His eyes darted to the family room where Mom was still on the phone. She didn't yell at us though. Except to say "Helmets!" which we snatched off the bench by the back door.

"Mission Dolores!" I hollered back, so she'd know where we were headed.

As we scooted down 18th Street, Flint yelled, "Holy Hands?" and Jabari looked at me. I gave a thumbs-up to the guys, and we turned up Church Street, away from the park. It's easier to practice in the parking lot there, as long as there aren't any cars. Saturdays are perfect.

We slid in and were going around pretty fast and hard. There's a little slope to the lot, so you can start at the far end and get a good bit of speed going before you have to turn.

As we caught our breath, I heard something that sounded like music. Jabari and Flint heard it, too, and we all grabbed our phones out of habit. Except Flint, who patted his pockets and looked panicked. Then he remembered and rolled his eyes.

But it wasn't a sound from our phones. Of course it wasn't, if we'd just thought about it. Who has a harmonica playing as a ring tone? Okay, maybe Flint, who one time *did* have some crazy banjo deal as a joke. But this sound was definitely a harmonica, and it was definitely coming from somewhere close by.

We kicked up our boards and walked a few steps together, following the sound. In the corner, where the lot meets the back side of the football field, there are a bunch of bushes and a narrow pathway with a fence on either side. We stepped around the bushes and onto the path and took a few steps. The space opened up just a little, and the music got louder at the same time. That's when we saw him.

He was thin but strong looking. I could see his muscles through his shirt, which looked like the tight layer I wear under my clothes when I go skiing with Flint's family. It was once white, but now it was more yellow and was streaked with dirt. A torn red-and-blue flannel shirt hung open in the front and was all he had for a jacket. He had bright brown eyes and a scruffy beard. The sunlight bounced off a silver chain around his neck, and I froze. I knew that wasn't just any necklace. It was dog tags.

But that wasn't all. At his feet beside his muddy boots was an actual dog.

We stared at each other for a minute. Even though he was a stranger and the dog had a pretty fierce wolf face—and they had clearly been hiding behind the bushes—I wasn't scared.

Jabari was another story. I looked at him, and it was almost like you could see STRANGER DANGER flashing across his face. Flint had bucked up a little bit, the only sign he had any worries. But he smiled.

"Hey. Sorry, man. Didn't mean to bust in to your … um … space. Just wanted to thank you for the concert."

The man held the harmonica in one hand and gave us a little salute with the other. "Thank you very much for that. It's pretty unusual for kids to like the blues.

Maybe there's hope for America after all." When he said that last part, he snorted a little bit. He was cracking himself up.

I just kept looking at the dog, which was positioned right beside him in a really strong, dignified way. He had long fur, sort of golden tan that spanned out at his neck like a lion's mane. Also, a long black nose. He looked at us with yellow brown eyes that almost matched his fur. They seemed to be glowing.

"May I pet your dog?" I asked.

Jabari drew in a breath. I don't know why I wasn't afraid. I just had a good feeling about it.

"He would certainly love that. Oh, sorry to be rude. This is Clyde. And I am James Arthur Bonnie III. But if you want me to answer, you'll call me Jazz."

I took a few steps closer and knelt down. The glowing eyes followed me. I reached out slowly and stroked Clyde's head, then ran my hand down his back. His fur was surprisingly soft. It felt like Mom's favorite sweater that she wears on special occasions. Cotton? Cashmere. Clyde's head rested into my hand, and he leaned his body toward me. What a good dog.

"Ha!" Jabari suddenly said. "I get it!"

We looked at him, startled. His face turned red. "I mean, I get the name. Clyde." He started to stammer at our blank faces. "You ... you know, the name Clyde. Because of James, I mean because of Jazz *Bonnie* ..." He looked a little unsure of himself then. "Bonnie and Clyde," he concluded quietly.

"Exactly!" the man Jazz said. "Definitely that version. Not so much Jay-Z and Beyoncé—we're not cool enough for that. But we are best friends. And a team to be reckoned with. And trouble, if you believe what some people say."

"But they're wrong about that?" Flint had bowed up again. Maybe I'm just dumb. But there wasn't anything about this man or this dog that seemed scary to me.

"They are absolutely wrong about it. We just aren't supposed to be staying here. But we don't have another option at this point. And this is not the worst place we could be, trust me on that. Of course, a few combat tours with the War on Terror in Iraq sets the bar real low." Jazz Bonnie laughed at himself again.

Jazz's tone became serious. "But back to your question. We aren't doing anything bad to anybody."

"You sleep here?" I asked. My skin had prickled a little when he said *Iraq*. I looked closer and saw a large drawstring bag behind Jazz. He'd been leaning up against it. It looked like the corners of a dirty pillow were sticking out from the opening. A small, plastic grocery bag was beside that, with a mix of wrappers and trash and a few wrapped crackers. A Snickers bar. A Styrofoam container.

"For the moment, yes. Sometimes in Dolores Park. Sometimes down the street. But this is our best spot by far."

I let that sink in for a moment.

"What about the Crown Hotel Shelter?" Jabari asked.

Leave it to Jabari to know the name of a shelter. Whenever we have to turn in our service hours for Honor Society, Jabari always folds his sheet before setting it in the bin. So no one can see he had double the required hours. I think he likes to go help around the city with his dad, who volunteers a lot. When he asked his question, he didn't sound weird or scared. He actually sounded interested.

"Ah, yes, the new hotel for old soldiers," Jazz Bonnie said, looping a couple of fingers around his tags. "Well. That isn't a bad spot. It's a good place to get a warm meal. And a hot shower. A lot of the guys like it there okay."

Once again, I felt this weighty feeling at the thought of *a lot* of Jazz Bonnies.

"But there's one very big problem with the Crown Hotel Shelter."

"Druggies and murderers?" Flint said.

Jabari closed his eyes, and I swatted him on the leg.

But Jazz Bonnie just laughed. "Well, maybe so, son," he said. "But no, that's not what I was thinking. It's a much worse problem than that."

I looked at Flint and J, and their eyes were as wide as mine. Worse than murderers?

But when I looked back at Jazz Bonnie, he wasn't looking at us. He was rubbing his hand down that gleaming, soft, cashmere back.

"The Crown would be an excellent place for me," he said. "But they won't take Clyde."

CHAPTER 12
FAMOUS

We didn't get on our boards even once on the way back to the house. We were too busy talking. About Jazz Bonnie. And Clyde the dog. Jabari thought we should definitely tell our parents about him.

"Yeah, sure, let's put it in the Holy Hands weekly email. So they can kick him out super fast and steal his dog. Great idea, J." Flint shook his head.

"But maybe there's a place where he can go and take Clyde," Jabari replied. "How can we help him if we don't know about that?"

"Maybe we should search the internet first. Just look and see if there are shelters that take pets," I said.

"Yeah, J, do some research before you start messing with the awesome Jazz Bonnie and the amazing Clyde-o," Flint said and punched lightly at Jabari.

"I do think he seems like a nice guy. That's why I want to help him. This plan of his isn't sustainable."

Flint and I looked at each other. It occurred to me that Jabari was the smartest of all of us. But once we told our parents, it'd be totally out of our hands. This sealed the deal for me. I remembered Jazz had said that not having Clyde was worse than murder. I didn't want to risk it.

"Okay. So how about this? Jabari searches the internet for the shelters. Flint and I bring Jazz and Clyde some stuff, like food and water and all. If he's not there, we can just leave it under that bush. So we'll know he's okay while we figure out what to do. And if there's a shelter that would take them both, I'll tell my mom about what happened."

"Go, Al-*bee*! Yaaaasssss. Like Abraham Lincoln said, 'Sometimes men see things as they are and ask why—I see things that never were and say why not.'"

Um, what?

Jabari threw his head back and let out a huge sigh. "Abraham Lincoln did *not* say that! Also, what does that have to do with Jazz Bonnie?"

"Well, I'm pretty sure he did," Flint said. "And it has to do with the fact that we didn't even know about Jazz Bonnie and Clyde the dog and now we do, and just because you don't know about a shelter for dogs and soldiers together doesn't mean there isn't one. Or shouldn't be one. Or that we shouldn't help them either way. *Dang.*"

Jabari looked at me, and I nodded. "Okay," he said as we walked up my back steps. "We'll do it your way."

"And just think—you have, like, another assignment to do! A research project. You must be so happy, J. That's what you call a win-win."

"Just so long as Abraham Lincoln didn't call it that," Jabari shot back.

We opened up the door and walked into the hallway. I rolled my board under the bench and set my helmet down on top of it. Jabari asked if he could have some water, and when I nodded he opened the cabinet and grabbed a glass and went to the sink. Flint went over to the counter to get his phone. Then he let out a little yelp.

"Whoa there, boys! I'm gettin' majorly no-tee-fied." He drawled out the last part of his word and started punching at his phone.

"Notifications?" Jabari asked. "From something you posted?" He followed Flint into the family room, and I jogged in behind J.

"Ah, yes. Yes, I am. And before we go any further, I'd like to say, surely we all agree that I should be designated Albert's PR guru, manager, and social secretary. For having the brains to put him into the Twitterverse."

"I don't really know what that means," I said. Great. It'd been nice not to think about the shark rescue for a little bit. And social media wasn't really my thing. Although looking at Flint's face, I wondered if I was missing out. I'd told people my mom and her rules were why I'm not on Snapchat and Instagram (Flint's the only one I know on Twitter, after his big sister set up an account to follow the kids from a Florida school where there was a shooting, and Flint begged his parents to get all the social media she had), even though she's pretty cool about that stuff. I just hadn't been that interested … before now.

"Let me show you what that means," Flint said, pulling out his phone dramatically. He tapped in his password, and when the screen opened up to his

Twitter, he cleared his throat like he was going to make a speech. He looked up at the ceiling and began talking in a loud voice.

"This here is my Twitter page, not a lot going on, just some skate stuff. That is, until Shark Kid came to life, saved a wild beast, became a media hero, and is now the star of my Twitter feed." He held it out and stepped up onto the ottoman. "In fact, my most popular video ever added to my media, even better than the well-liked boarding fail documentary, is the Albert Christian Davidson Shark Rescue, which is currently liked by a mere ..." He looked down, and then his head popped back quickly.

He held the phone out and then pulled it closer. He started shaking his head, peering into the screen.

"By a mere ... what? Is Albert not getting the love? You know, it's okay, Flint. I think he can handle it," Jabari laughed.

"He ... he *is* getting the love," Flint said slowly.

"So what's the problem?" I asked. "Did something bad happen on Twitter?" I thought of all the lectures I'd heard about social media. I felt a little flip in my stomach.

"Uh, no. Nothing bad ... but something did happen. I'm just not sure *what* exactly."

Jabari gave Flint a little push. "Come on, Bo, stop with the suspense. You're killing us here! How many likes did the video get?"

"Okay, okay!" Flint took a breath. "It got fourteen thousand likes."

The room was totally quiet. Then Jabari and I both started shouting at once. Fourteen *thousand*? J gave me a high-five and I just started laughing. I thought of a classroom at Holy Hands with twenty kids in it and how that felt crowded some days. *Fourteen thousand?*

"Oh man! Incredible! But ... how is that possible? No offense," J said, looking at me. When he saw my expression, he started laughing again. He clapped his hand on my shoulder.

Flint was punching on his phone, trying to make sense of it. His brow furrowed, and his eyes darted up and down, reading. His mouth dropped open.

"Uh, boys. I think I figured it out," he said slowly.

"Okay, what is it?" I asked.

"My tweet with your video was liked—and retweeted—by @Pontifex," Flint said. Jabari and I looked at him blankly.

"Albert!" he hollered, dropping the phone to grab both my shoulders and look at me square in the face. He smiled and shook his head at me and at confused Jabari. Something seemed to come over him as he held onto me, and his grip became firmer but calmer somehow too. His eyes were lit up like sparklers.

"Albie," Flint said. His voice was softer, but excited just the same. "Pope Francis retweeted that tweet."

WINTER

CHAPTER 13
A LINE BETWEEN OKAY AND NOT OKAY

I've learned that there are different kinds of celebrity and that with social media, celebrity is actually contagious. So, on one end you have Pope Francis, who obviously is a huge deal. People from all over the world know who he is. Then on the other end there's me, who until my Twitter fame was a complete nobody. Outside of my family and my friends and my school, anyway.

When you have a superstar celebrity touch something from a nobody, all of a sudden, it's like that thing gets shot full of water gushing out of a hose, filling it up with followers and interest and attention. That's what happened to me and the Shark Kid stuff.

I can't decide how I feel about it. It feels weird saying that I'm any kind of celebrity when I'm just the same as I've always been. Maybe it's better just to say that after that, I was known. Mom became a lot more protective of me and worried about the attention. I didn't want to stress her out. Who knew how long it would last and what would come of it. But it wasn't all bad having kids at school ask me about it and to be known for something like that. It was a nice distraction in some ways.

Especially once the holidays were here. Thanksgiving was pretty cool—Uncle Wood came and stayed with us, and he always makes things fun. I could tell that my mom felt better just having him around. Honestly, I did too. And the holiday season served up the chance for another distraction, Jazz Bonnie and his lion-dog, Clyde. I knew Jazz got a nice dinner at the church for Thanksgiving. Mom and I had decided to volunteer there since her medicine made her not want to eat much. I kept my face solid when I saw him walk in, and didn't let on that we knew each other. As he stood up to leave after his meal, he nodded at me and opened his coat just a little to show the secret pockets inside that he'd filled with leftovers. I'm thinking that back at the bush, Clyde was definitely thankful. I was glad they were able to have a good meal.

I seem to have a connection on a different level with Jazz than my friends do. Maybe it's more like me to be open to people in general. I don't have Jabari's "healthy fear" or Flint's fighter instinct. It's like when I look at someone, I really feel them somehow. Okay, that sounds pretty dumb. Maybe I just really like Jazz and Clyde.

I'm sure it has to do with the dog. I've always wanted one. But when we first moved into our house and Uncle Wood lived there (really, we moved into his house) and he was allergic, that was it. And then it just seemed too hard to add a dog into the mix, with Mom working

at the college so much and with me in school. I had
a guinea pig once named Trucks, but that's really not
the same.

Clyde is the coolest dog I've ever seen. Something
about him was very fierce looking. I think it was those
golden eyes and that big dark nose. "German Shepherd,"
Jazz had replied after I nuzzled it and said it was a
perfect length. He had walked over to where I'd been
sitting with Clyde and pulled his ears straight up. Once
they weren't tan and floppy and stood up over his eyes
and nose, it was super clear what breed he looked like.
From the neck up.

"Where'd you get him?" I'd asked, unpacking a bunch
of snacks that J and Flint had passed to me to bring to
Jazz. Granola bars and Lance crackers and Goldfish. The
Pahlavis always have a ton of stuff—I think J's sisters
are always hungry.

"We found each other," Jazz Bonnie said. A lot of
times when I asked questions, he didn't give actual
answers. But he was always very nice about it. And
really, was any of it my business? Just because I had a
connection with his dog didn't mean that Jazz had to tell
me everything. And my other connection with Jazz made
me want him to keep pretty quiet.

That is, Iraq. I hadn't told Jazz about my dad. I don't
really know why. But it just seems better to keep that to
myself. I think it might be too hard for Jazz. Sometimes
he would say something about the war or being in the
Army or the desert, and you could see that he was so,
so sad. Once I came up on him when he was sleeping,
and he cried out. I wasn't sure if I should touch him. I

ended up leaving and not doing anything. There's a line between okay and not okay, and I didn't want to cross it.

But there were really great times too. The best was when Flint and Jabari and I had circled up with Jazz at Dolores Park. Those hills are so big and wide, and there's always fun stuff going on over there. We'd gone there first and planned to stop by the lot on the way back, but then we heard the harmonica. It was pretty cool how Jazz could play it. We followed the sound like we had that first day and finally saw him over by the tennis courts, with Clyde at his feet.

"Probably not the smartest move to be making a lot of noise near your school, right boys?" he'd said.

We agreed that was right. But I was glad he had figured out another way to play. I thought of my art and how it would feel if I couldn't draw or make anything. I think I need to do it the most when times are hard. So I was glad Jazz had figured out a way to keep his music with him.

With Christmas coming up, I want to get the perfect present for Jazz and Clyde. At first, I didn't know what that was. Then I passed the consignment shop on my way home from Mission Skate. They had a ton of stuff in the window. I decided to go in.

Some people might think that place is a mess. Or, *Gross, this stuff isn't new and someone else had it first.* I didn't feel that way though. I always thought it was pretty solid that cool treasures lasted from one person to the next.

When I walked inside, there was almost too much to take in. But once I started looking around, I got used to how packed all the space was. I could pretty much see everything in there. And then I spotted it. There was a red bag and then a smaller bag next to it that looked the same. I opened up the larger one, and the lightest sleeping bag ever popped out. It was shiny and soft and folded up into nothing. The smaller bag was for a kid, but it was made of the same thing. Both bags together were twenty dollars.

I grabbed them and started to head back over to the register to pay. I was trying to get around a big table and a stack of books when I heard it. There was no mistaking that voice. Usually it made me smile, but today I just froze—and hoped she wasn't heading my way.

"So then I told her, I think I'm gonna have to go back to school if Flint needs any more help with his math homework. How depressing is that? I mean, it's seventh grade—"

And Big Anne turned the corner and ran right into me. She looked startled and then broke into a big smile.

"Well, hey there, Albert! Sure didn't expect I'd run into you here! This is my friend, Angie Greene. Angie, this is one of Flint's best friends."

I dropped the bags and held out my hand, my mind racing before the next question. "Nice to meet you."

"Nice to meet *you*. Wow, manners! Refreshing."

"Oh, yes, honey. That's the Southern in him, am I right, Albie?"

"Uh, yes, ma'am," I felt my face turn red. I stepped in front of my bags and tried to block them from view. Unfortunately, that did the opposite. Big Anne glanced down at my feet and saw the presents.

"Surprised to see you here. Flint would be a bull in a china shop in a place like this. Shopping?" she asked, looking pointedly at the floor.

"No. I mean, yes. Well, one of the guys at Mission Skate is taking his daughter camping this weekend. They don't have bags. But I pass this store almost every day and remembered they were in the window. He gave me the money, and I got them for him."

It did feel a little bad to lie right to Big Anne's face. But I had to protect Jazz and Clyde.

Mrs. Greene smiled. "Polite and so nice too."

Ugh. Double dose of guilt. I needed to get out of there before this got worse.

Big Anne was peeking into the outer bags and laughed a bit when she saw what was inside. "Clever," she remarked.

"Yes, it should work great. Okay, well. Have a good one." I grabbed the bags and raced up to the counter. I was so glad there wasn't a line. As I busted out of the store, I looked back through the front glass window. Big Anne smiled and waved.

I couldn't wait to get these gifts to Jazz Bonnie and Clyde, and not only because of that run-in. I tucked them under my bed when I got home and then raced over to the back lot the first chance I got. I carried the bag strings looped together around my shoulders, with a red bow I found with Mom's wrapping stuff on top of the big one.

When I turned the corner to Jazz's bush, he jumped out right in front of me. It was so hard and so quick that he almost knocked me over. I let out a little shout, and his hand went over my mouth.

It all happened so fast—I looked up at him, my eyes wide. His eyes seemed strange, like they were looking but not really seeing. It was like he was looking over me. But then he looked down. I saw his big brown eyes focus. He let me go.

"Albert! I ... I'm sorry. Are you okay?" He was breathing hard. He bent in half and put his hands on his knees.

"I'm fine," I said. Even I didn't believe it. My mind was racing to make sense of what he'd done. It was completely out of control.

"Look, I'm sorry, kid. I don't really know what to say. I just, I had a bad dream or something. It seemed like maybe someone was coming to hurt me. But in fact, the opposite seems to be true." He was looking at my bags.

"Oh, yeah, no that's fine. It's okay." I wasn't sure who I was trying to convince. I thought about Jabari wanting us to tell our parents about Jazz and Clyde. Maybe I don't have such a great sense about people after all.

But then I handed him his early Christmas present, and his face just sort of melted. In a good way. His eyes got big and wet. He pulled out the sleeping bags and laughed when he saw the kid one for Clyde. Honestly, I think the fact that I had brought the same gift for the dog did something to him. Some people might be insulted by that. For him it was the opposite.

"Albert. It's perfect. Thank you, son." He smoothed his hand over the bag and then patted it. Clyde got up and circled around the material, sniffing. Then he stretched out across it and put his head down. I sat with him for a while and petted that soft, silky fur. Jazz Bonnie sat on the other side and petted him too.

"You know, this is truly the most thoughtful gift I have ever received," he said.

It made me feel good. He was fine. Better than fine. I decided it was best to keep what happened at this visit to myself. I'd probably overreacted before. In fact, I started to get a little bit into the Christmas spirit. Which was a good thing, this year especially.

Mom's treatment schedule worked out so that we could go see Uncle Wood in Charleston over Christmas, and that's something cool to look forward to. That trip is dangling in front of me like a shiny ornament, and I just keep my eyes on the prize. Because certain times of the year are always harder without my dad, and Christmas is one of them.

CHAPTER 14

THE GOODBYE TREE

For most of December I decided that the best strategy was to try to keep things light. Early Christmas presents for Jazz and Clyde had been part of that idea. Which hadn't started out so good but had ended up according to plan. And it seemed like maybe another good thing when Jabari asked if I would go with him to take his sisters to see Santa at the mall.

Actually, though, this was a little complicated. Jabari's sisters make me tired. Maybe I'm too used to the quiet since there are no other kids in my family but me. But it always seems like his sisters are speaking to someone with a hearing problem—they shriek all of their words. They also will randomly burst into songs for no apparent reason. They are always gabbing about some show, unless they are fighting. Their fights are epic. Those girls wear me out.

But Jabari doesn't really have a choice about it. He only has one "chore" at home, and that is to help out with his sisters. So, he's stuck. And as far as that gig could go, having to be at the mall wasn't too bad a deal.

And none of that was as important as wanting to make sure J was okay after what had happened at school last week. Pat outdid himself. Although I don't know why I'm ever surprised by Pat's meanness. Or that he has an especially unfortunate thing for J.

But this day had been next level, even for Pat. That morning I saw him stop by the trophy case in the front of the school by the office and lean against the wall waiting for the early bell. He squinted his eyes in this ugly way, watching Jabari's grandmother come into the school quickly behind J and hand him something he had left in the car. She gave him a quick kiss on the cheek and then went out as fast as she'd come in. I kept walking to class and didn't think too much about it.

Apparently, Jabari had smiled looking down at the clock he'd built all on his own at home. He was pumped his grandmother brought it after he left it in the car accidentally. He had wanted to show it to Mr. Nelson, the advisor of the engineering club. He turned it over in his hands and rubbed the face against his jacket to polish it a bit.

And that's when Pat went berserk. He started hollering and pointing at J. "A bomb! He's got a bomb!"

He ran over and knocked it out of Jabari's hand. It crashed to the floor and shattered. It was so stupid and so crazy, but people started buzzing around. A few started running. Father Russo came out of the office with Principal Gersin just then and took in the scene, poor Jabari with the clock in pieces at his feet and his mouth open. Pat acting like Pat. Which probably saved the day. Because it took all of one half of one second to decide who was the problem. Mr. Gersin snatched the back of Pat's jacket and hauled him into the office.

News of this stupid mess traveled fast at school. When I could finally ask J about it later in second period study hall, I was so mad.

"When is someone going to do something real about that guy? This is ridiculous!"

And then Jabari told me maybe the worst part. That he'd been sitting on a bench beside the secretary's desk, waiting to talk to Gersin, when Pat's dad came to get him. He'd been suspended for the rest of the week. I thought of how much trouble I'd be in with Mom if that ever happened to me. I guessed that Pat's dad went ballistic. But J shook his head.

"No. No, not at all. The opposite, in fact." He looked down. "He wasn't in trouble. His dad gave him a big hug. Went in and yelled at Mr. Gersin. Then left with his arm around Pat like he couldn't be prouder."

Jabari's face fell even more. I didn't know what to say to make it better. People can be so messed up.

But now there was something I could do. Jabari is a good friend. Who had a really bad week. I decided to go to the mall.

"Hey, it's the Shark Kid!" the girls shrieked when I climbed into the car, before I could even say hi to Jabari's dad, who was dropping us off. Then they started making sounds like the music from the old *Jaws* movie.

"*Da* dum ... *Da* dum ... dadumdadumdadum!" They laughed and fell against each other and then started to do a cheer of some sort that ended with words that sounded a lot like a Lady Gaga song.

I gave J a long look. He blushed.

"Sorry, man. Hey! Dial it down, will ya? Albert's never gonna want to go anywhere with us again!"

"Sorry, Albert," the girls sang together.

"Yes, sorry, Albert," Mr. Pahlavi said. "To make it up to you, next time I'll take you by my new project. We have some extra materials I think you'd like."

Mr. Pahlavi is an amazing architect who designs the wildest buildings. His last project turned a run-down complex into one of the coolest places in San Francisco. The city is helping to keep the rent low so lots of people can afford to live there. I couldn't wait to get my hands on any leftovers he might have.

"Deal!" I said and smiled at J's sisters, who giggled and smiled back.

When we got to the mall, tons of people were streaming in the front doors. A song blasted from a speaker outside, but different music was playing inside once we stepped through the entryway. It almost sounded like an indoor carnival. I passed the Sunglass Hut and JCrew and then coughed as J's sisters let some lady at a makeup booth spray them with perfume. Christmas decorations hung in every store entrance, and silver and gold sparkly streamers ran down the walls. There was so much coming at you at once. If I wanted a distraction, this was it. Except right near where the Santa line was forming, they had the mac-daddy Christmas tree up and completely decorated and blinking with all of these bright lights. I walked over to it.

As I stood in front of it, it was like someone had pressed a mute button on all of the noise around me. It was like when water gets in your ear or you hold a seashell up to it—just a muffled background but not the main thing. The main thing was this massive tree. Even though the point of being at the mall was to be distracted from feeling down, I could tell that the Christmas overload was actually starting to make me feel bad. And then here was this tree.

I could feel my stomach tighten and my heart pound. I needed a strategy, but no pictures came to my mind. I thought of the last time I had checked in with Sister and we had talked about how I could use prayer as a strategy. I tried it now—not the whole thing, just the part from the Prayer of Saint Francis that helps me. *Lord make me an instrument of your peace. Hatred ... love. Injury ... pardon. Doubt ... faith. Despair ... hope.*

I repeated the opposite words a few times and was calmer each time I said them in my head. I felt a little guilty that I had never thought to try prayers first as a strategy. I pushed the guilty feeling away. I just wanted to feel okay. I looked up at the massive branches with all of their jumbo-sized sparkling ornaments and tinsel.

Every time I see a tree that stands out in some way, I think of my dad. This is a big deal for the obvious reason that since my dad is gone, anything that makes me think of him is important. But it's a lot more than that. Trees were my thing with my dad. So it would make sense that he would say goodbye to me with a tree.

I don't remember a whole lot about my dad since I was only four when he died. But there are certain things that pop out at me sometimes. Like his big boots. Or his really short hair and clean-shaven face. I can remember rubbing my hands on the top of his head and on his stubbly cheeks. Or putting my cheek up to his and pressing against his skin.

I remember he loved movies, and when he was home with us he had always wanted to have movie night. I would fall asleep when we were watching them. Really, they had probably not been exactly right for me because they were grown-up movies. But I don't think I'd really understood any of that. I just liked to curl up between my parents and fall asleep while they watched and laughed.

The strongest memory I have of my dad was climbing this tree at the park around the corner from our apartment where we'd lived near the base. I think we must have done it all the time when he was home. There is a picture of my dad in that tree with me as a baby strapped inside some baby backpack that you wear backward so it holds the baby in the front. He is laughing and holding on to the branches with me strapped in. Mom says she was totally freaking out when she took that picture. Maybe my dad was laughing at her a little bit. But my point is that we were in the trees from before I could even walk.

And once I was able to really move around on my own, I used to love to climb. Just like my dad. One time my parents couldn't find me, and it was because I had climbed the shelves that went all the way up the wall in my bedroom. I was just sitting up there at the top in my diaper, laughing and swinging my legs over the edge. That was another time when my mom had not been feeling the Davidson climbing genes. But Dad got me. He took the picture that time, while my mom screamed and ran around in circles like a crazy person.

My mom and dad loved a movie called *Phenomenon,* and they watched it sometimes when my dad had been home. He had the CD to that movie in the car, and we would listen to it, and he would talk about the different scenes in the movie that went along with the song that was playing. He'd make it really simple and like something a little kid would understand. He was a great storyteller. And his favorite part of the movie was when George talked about how the trees were all connected and part of all living things, and we were all part of them too.

When my dad was working, I did not get to climb very much. Maybe that's why I remember that part so well, because even though I was small, I always wanted to climb. I could feel a pull so strong when I wasn't able to. And how happy I was when I could! And when my dad was deployed, my mom and I would still go to the park, but only to play on the playground or dig in the sandbox or walk around the pond. I would pass my dad's tree, and some days it would make me really down. Then again, some days it would make me feel like he was right there with me, like my very own *Phenomenon* tree.

But the saddest thing with our tree happened when my dad died.

He'd already been gone for a long time overseas, and it was hard on Mom. She was obsessed with the news.

And then she would not want to watch it at all. I didn't understand much about the specifics of what my dad did. But I knew he was a soldier. I knew he was brave. I knew he was far away when he was gone from us, and I knew that where he was there was sand everywhere. But I didn't know words like *Iraq* or *terror* or *surge*. I've learned all about that since then. I was only a little kid back then, and there was a lot that was kept from me because I was too young to understand.

Still, I guessed that my dad was having to be really brave because of how worried Mom was. She kept taking me to the park, and we would see our tree. And one day, we were there, and it was really sunny and nice. It was not windy, and it wasn't storming. And for no reason that anyone can explain, on this one day when we were at the park and I was looking at the tree and thinking of my dad, all of a sudden there was this horrible noise. It sounded like when a bat hits a ball at a baseball game, but it was a long sound, like *craaaaaaaack*. As we heard this crazy noise, we realized it was coming from the tree. And one whole side of it—two big branches that connected together at the trunk—just split apart. It was like it had been struck by lightning or attacked by a tornado, but there was nothing like that anywhere. The other moms at the park hollered and grabbed their kids. And my mom grabbed me. It could've been really bad if someone had been climbing it or playing around it. But no one was there. As we all watched, the branches cracked away, and half the tree fell to the ground with a *whooooosh*. The branches were so heavy and so long that when they landed, they smashed part of the metal fence that went around the sandbox and the swings. Just crushed it to the ground.

It was awful. But it wasn't until a few days later that it made sense to me. Because by then, we had learned that there had been some really terrible things happening in Iraq. There were a lot of roadside bombs that went off and a lot of fighting, and it was even more dangerous than usual. Many of the soldiers did not make it. And my dad was one of those guys.

And that's when I knew. I knew it like you know something deep inside. Something you can't explain. But you know it's real. My dad hadn't wanted to leave me. He had not wanted to die. He had fought as hard as he could, but then he got hurt real bad. He had become broken in a way that could not be fixed. And he had known it.

They say that when you are dying, your whole life flashes before your eyes, and I think when his got to Mom and me, Dad got furious at what was happening. He would be gone and not able to ever see us again. To watch a movie or climb with me. He would not even be able to say goodbye.

So many years later when Sister read that Dylan Thomas poem at the assembly at Holy Hands, I knew. Dad did not go gentle. He raged against leaving us. His sadness and his anger and his fighting for his life broke our tree. I believe this more than anything else. When I was four years old, I wouldn't have been able to explain it like I am now. But even then, I knew my dad and that tree breaking apart had been connected. Like how you might not understand gravity, but you know that if you drop something, it will fall. The moment those branches broke away and fell to the ground, my dad was really gone.

So when I saw this huge Christmas tree in the mall, I felt so many things at once. It was tough and sad but sort of sweet too. It's hard to explain. I noticed that the girls were pulling on Jabari, and he was watching me with a worried look. I must've looked upset, and he probably would have guessed a bunch of reasons why, but I'm sure he wouldn't ever think it was because I was wrecked by a Christmas tree. I shook my head and I made myself smile. All around us a million shoppers walked by, talking and laughing and buying things for Christmas. No one else looked sad to me.

I needed to get out of my head. I walked up to J and said, "Let's do this."

I directed the hyper girls around the green giant and down the red velvet ropes. We walked a long way until we finally reached the back side of the food court. Even as far back as we were, I could still see the Christmas tree. It was okay, though. A warm feeling came over me like a blanket and kept me solid. We joined all the others in a line that snaked up and down the huge mall— tons of people waiting, but that's no surprise. If there's a special chance to get something you really want, of course you have to try to take it.

CHAPTER 15
DIVE IN + MAKE A DIFFERENCE

've always been glad when the New Year comes. The end of the year wears me out. There's the part where I really miss my dad. There's all the craziness of the stores and the busy way people move around the streets. The whole month of December makes me think of the commercials you fast-forward through on a show you've DVR'd. Times two, times three, times four—faster and faster and faster.

Even with all of the busyness, some things were guaranteed to slow me and Mom down. Chemo, although it wasn't too bad this time. We had that drill figured out pretty well. School work. I was working on a cool mixed-media project in art that I really liked, but it was taking up a lot of time. Instead of a canvas, I used a piece of wood from Lands End and hammered a thousand nails into it, painting them green to make the leaves of trees, and then super-glued a big piece of blue glass to the bottom to make it look like water. At least working on that assignment made me feel calm and happy. Not so much my massive science paper (the problem with your science teacher and your English teacher being the same person). On top of that, all of the craziness with the shopping and music and holiday stuff everywhere you turned. It was intense. At least as soon as we were out of school and Mom was feeling strong enough, we got to fly to see Uncle Wood in Charleston.

Well, actually, in a place at the beach outside of Charleston called Wild Dunes. It's a cool spot where we've stayed the past several years. The condos Uncle Wood rents are over a boardwalk where there are good restaurants and an awesome mini-grocery with amazing candy and milkshakes and sandwiches. At night they have a fire pit and music and movies on the lawn. Even though it's too cold to swim, we can play tennis and bike on the trails and walk on the beach. It's wild to think that I live by the Pacific Ocean and Uncle Wood lives by the Atlantic Ocean and that our country is right in between. That trip is usually my favorite present I get at Christmas.

But this year something beat the Wild Dunes extravaganza. It's tied for my favorite gift ever, with my Oris Hart original tree-art skateboard. Although getting this latest best gift didn't start out so well at first.

Because whenever I talked to Jabari and Flint about whether we were exchanging gifts, they would act really weird. They'd give each other these strange looks. One would start to speak and then the other would talk over him. I couldn't understand the drama. It wasn't a given that we'd give each other presents—some years we would just go get food someplace and hang out and call it a

Merry Christmas. Or we'd go to the movies and stuff our faces with candy and popcorn. But some years, we had given each other a little something. One year we all gave each other gift certificates to Mission Skate, which was pretty funny. It really didn't matter to me which way we decided to go. I just wanted to know ahead of time so I'd know what to do.

But they were being pretty annoying about it. After I asked for the tenth time what our plan was, I got back, "Uh, yeah, that's a negative, bro," from Flint at the same moment Jabari said, "Sure! Let's do something this year." After which Flint promptly punched J in the arm. Hard. They looked at each other in a way that made me feel like I was left out of a joke. It didn't feel good.

That was all forgotten, though, when Mom and I went over to the Petersons for dinner the night that school let out for the holidays. As soon as we opened the door, we heard a bunch of people yell "Surprise!" Behind Flint and Big Anne, I could see Jabari and his parents and Sister and even Father Russo and Principal Gersin. I jumped and so did Mom. I'm sure we looked pretty funny. Who was the surprise party for? Baby Jesus? My birthday was in July. Mom's was in May.

Just then Jabari's sisters came busting up to us wearing skateboarding helmets, except they had been changed so they had a shark's fin sticking up on the top. They looked so funny crashing through the group. Once they got up to us, they handed us shark-tooth necklaces. That's when I noticed there was a banner strung up across the back wall: SAVE-

THE-SHARK SKATEBOARDING CHALLENGE FUNDRAISER FOR CANCER RESEARCH."

And that's how we learned that their Christmas present to me and Mom was planning and lining up a most-awesome event to take place in January to help raise money for rare cancers like Mom's. It was the nicest thing anyone had ever done for us— and since Mom got sick, people had done a lot of nice stuff.

I knew I was always a little checked out in December, but this proved I was really out of it. All of this was going on behind the scenes, and except for our gift-giving mystery, I hadn't had a clue. And there'd been a bunch of details to figure out. It was hilarious when Flint and J broke it all down for me. First off, there had been some fights about what to call this thing. Flint had come up with Save-the-Shark, which Jabari thought was off-base. Flint argued that the Shark Kid Twitter account had thousands of followers, and I was basically famous for saving the shark and that was the coolest thing in life and the best theme ever. Exhibit A: dorsal-fin helmets and shark-tooth necklaces.

"Sure, but will people think they are giving money to save sharks?" Jabari had asked.

"Who cares? They're giving money—it's for a good cause. They'll get over it," Flint had responded while J shook his head and sighed.

Finally, Sister had worked out a deal. "Look, guys, I think it's very catchy. But what does "Save-the-Shark" mean? Why that metaphor? If you can convince me, then we'll keep it."

Flint had worked this over in his head for a few minutes. Then he said, "When Albert saved the shark near Lands End that day, he saw a problem and did what he could to try to fix it. It was hard and risky, but he took a chance and ended up doing something really cool."

Jabari and Sister had both looked pretty stunned with his answer. And impressed.

"Wow," J said, then laughed at Flint's startled expression.

Flint had been pretty surprised himself with what had come out of his own mouth.

"*Love* it!" Sister had yelled. "As you boys know, I can totally rock a good theme. I'll be making a Facebook page immediately. But the bells and whistles aren't as important as the larger point. It has to make sense."

And with that directive, the whole amazing plan was hatched. That "Save-the-Shark" would be followed by "Dive in & Make a Difference," plus, just to be clear, "Fundraiser for Cancer Research."

The best part was that the whole thing would revolve around a skateboarding challenge. Before the event, teams and individuals would get sponsors to make donations that translated into their skate time during the fundraiser. Boarders who wanted to increase their donations could announce a "Save-the-Shark challenge" of a new trick they wanted to try or a jump they wanted to do, if a certain donation amount was raised. This morphed into kids challenging each other. If you didn't want to do the challenge, you would donate instead or get pledges to cover your pass. Mission Skate offered to judge the skating part and to give prizes from the shop to the winners of the event.

Once Mom and I were in on the deal, things really took off. The Save-the-Shark idea started making its way over our texts. And then onto YouTube and TikTok. Kids sure like to see themselves online. But all this media exposure was only helping our cause. As it grew, it also started to change.

Dori Martin didn't like to skate, but she loved to climb. A week before the fundraiser, she filmed herself at Inner Peaks in front of the tallest wall I have ever seen, with random tiny pieces of colored putty sticking out from it. How anyone could figure out how to turn those random pieces into steps was completely crazy to me. I remembered when Pat was so mean to her when school first started. No way could he ever get up that wall. It looked impossible.

But she filmed herself in front of it and said, "I'm going to scale this wall for the Save-the-Shark fundraiser. It scares me so much! But what I need to climb this wall is probably half the bravery you need when you're getting chemo. So for fifty dollars I will 'save this shark!'"

She got a bunch of text pledges and before long had the money she had asked for. She then gave her phone to someone at Inner Peaks to film her as she started up the wall.

She made quick time up the first third of it, grabbing the lumps with her hands and wedging her feet into the tiniest of cracks and ledges. It was pretty impressive. I was surprised that I had never known that she climbed. I guess everyone has a thing.

But then she got stuck. She tried one side and then another. Each time her foot would hold for a moment but then give way. Once she slipped so hard, she fell away from the wall and then slammed back into it. She tilted her head up, and I saw her back expand with a huge breath. Her hands went up to her face, and I wondered if she was crying. It looked terrible. She was pretty high up. Her legs were shaking either from being so tired or from being scared. It was actually hard to watch.

She shook her whole body in this determined kind of way. She slapped her hands back onto the gray surface. She stared at the knobs for a moment and then started moving very slowly up. When her foot started to slip, she pressed her body forward and stayed solid. Soon she was past the tricky part. It was wild that the last part was actually a faster climb than the middle. When she got to the top, she rang the bell a million times. Her smile was huge and pretty goofy after she popped back down and unbuckled. What she had done was very, very cool.

This substitute type of challenge took off like wildfire. A group of girls held yoga planks for a gazillion minutes to "save the shark." Afterward they lined up and did a little yoga pose bow and said, "Namaste," but instead of having their hands together at their chests, they had them together on their heads to look like a shark. Somebody started making shark-themed T-shirts, and they'd show up in some of the videos. Sister then organized a T-shirt contest for the kids at school, and I was all over that. Carlos from drama club posted a really wild, spoken-word poem all about swimming with the sharks. It was amazing.

So this was unlike any January before in my entire life. When I had my check-in with Sister, I sat on the bench behind the science building at school and just gabbed about the skateboarding tricks I planned to do for my part of the event. Sister teased that when she showed Mom the T-shirts from our contest, "for some reason" she loved the one I designed (and signed) the best. It's kinda embarrassing to admit that I didn't really talk about Mom's chemo even one time, even though she had been really pale and tired lately. I couldn't wait for the third Saturday to come when the actual Save-the-Shark Challenge was scheduled at Potrero Del Sol, one of the best skateboarding parks in the city.

CHAPTER 16
SKATEBOARDING EXTRAVAGANZA

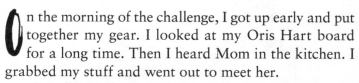

On the morning of the challenge, I got up early and put together my gear. I looked at my Oris Hart board for a long time. Then I heard Mom in the kitchen. I grabbed my stuff and went out to meet her.

"Hey, hon." She turned to me when I walked in. She was wearing the cool T-shirt I had designed that had a funny cartoon shark skateboarding over the Golden Gate Bridge. She laughed when she saw me checking it out.

"Nice! Glad to see you dressed up," I joked. The T-shirt really did have awesome colors. It made me feel happy just looking at it. Mom looked pretty wearing it.

"Sister showed me a bunch that I could pick from. Apparently, there was some kind of contest? It's just been amazing what you kids have come up with. Of course, this one was the clear winner." She ran her palm across my initials at the bottom and winked at me.

"So much about this event blows my mind. All of the students participating. And Sister and the teachers at Holy Hands. You know, they did a lot behind the scenes so you guys could do this. And all the money! They set up a 501(c)(3)."

Seeing my face, she explained, "A nonprofit, a charity. They've done a lot of work so you guys could have all the glory."

She reached over and tousled my hair. I let her. It had gotten pretty long. Haircuts weren't on top of the to-do list these days.

"I've spoken with the folks over at UCSF Medical Center," she said. "They already have doctors on staff and projects that the contest money will fund directly. Pretty exciting."

Her eyes got a little teary and she added, "I'm really proud of you, Albert."

I smiled at her. It felt so good to be combining all of these things that I loved to do with something that would help her. Raising the money to get better medicines and treatments and cures for her cancer. Which today you might not even believe she had, just looking at her.

"Okay, don't freak out," she said in a kind of exaggerated way. "But there may be a little tiny bit of rain today. But just a teeny bit! And maybe not at all. But either way, make sure you have your hoodie. It's chilly."

Even that bit of bad news didn't get me down. And it seemed like my good attitude was rewarded. By the time we left the house, the sun was shining, and it was pretty out. It seemed like a good sign.

As we entered the park, we could hear music playing. A DJ was set up on the grass, and a bunch of kids were dancing in front of his speakers. There were balloons and food and hand-painted banners everywhere. Bins overflowed with dorsal-fin hats and shark-tooth necklaces for anyone who wanted to take them. A bunch of parents and teachers had blankets and chairs set up over to the side. Mom went over to give Sister a big hug. Leave it to Sister to know how to give a huge hug that was also gentle—I could see her carefully hold Mom, who was so skinny now. You could hear laughing and talking and all kinds of noise. And, of course, the sound of wheels on pavement, trucks catching metal rims, the smacking sound of boards hitting the ground. A different kind of music, you might say.

Mission Skate had a table set up over to the side. I took a big swig of Gatorade and watched the teams starting to gather and check in. I scanned the crowd for Flint and J. Suddenly I saw Pat McBee and his crew. My mouth fell open. I couldn't believe that they'd show up here to wreck things. No *way* was I going to let that happen. I could feel my back and neck tense up, and I grabbed my board tighter.

But then I looked closer. I saw Pat signing in and putting on his shark-tooth necklace. He caught me watching him, and nodded in my direction. Pat's crew ran up to him and he started pointing out where we'd skate. I blinked hard. What was I seeing? Was he actually going to try to help today? That was a pretty wild thought. What were the chances? I took another swig of my drink and calmed down. This wasn't the day to feel mad. This was a day for good things. The vibe in the park was very cool and fun.

Everyone looked pretty pumped. Kids were starting to practice on their boards. As I watched them, someone smacked my back. I turned around and saw Flint. And promptly spit my Gatorade out onto the pavement.

"Uh, hi Smurf Man," I said after I recovered a little bit.

Flint was wearing a shiny blue bodysuit that covered him from head to toe. He looked just like one of the guys from the Blue Man Group. He'd cut out crazy eyeholes on the face so he could see. The outfit was topped off with a shark-fin helmet that had been spray-painted silver.

"Shark Man! The most totally awesome and wonderful Shark Man mascot ready to get this party started! Get it straight, A. D. I'll win best-looking if nothing else today!"

Jabari jogged up to us then. His eyes got wider and wider as he got closer to Flint.

"Papa Smurf?" he said once he got to us.

"Ya'll are *killing* me! You'd think you'd be smart enough to dress out today."

"Right. We're the dumb ones. Got it," Jabari retorted, reaching over to pluck the shiny bodysuit material.

"Guys! We have to get ready to do this. I think we open the show. And actually, Bo, this will be a very strong start."

Suddenly I had the same feeling I had when I saw Dori climb the wall. Granted, Flint liked being the center of attention a lot of the time. But this costume—shiny, bright, ridiculous, fun—it took something to put yourself out there like that.

As it turned out, Flint wasn't the only one who'd put himself out there. When I pointed out Pat and his crew to Jabari, he didn't look worried. Or even surprised.

"Yeah, I know," he said. He tipped his head and looked at me sideways. "I'm the reason they're here."

"What do you mean?"

"Mr. Gersin wanted some suggestions as to how Pat should make things right after he broke my clock." He pressed his lips together a little bit.

And said you were a terrorist bomber, I thought, a hot feeling filling my chest. But like J, I didn't say anything about that.

Jabari's thin lips spread into a smile. "As part of his reconciliation, we came up with this."

Flint snorted. "Whoa—you mean you got to think up punishments? How about crawl to class every day carrying your books? How about getting a tattoo that says "Pahlavi Rocks"? How about a hundred Hail Marys and fifty push-ups every time he wants to speak?" Flint was getting going. "Man, you shoulda talked to me!"

"Well, I did think about it a little. I can't lie—it'd be satisfying to make him feel a little pain. But then where does it end? I wanted to show him a different way. And help Albie," Jabari blushed a little bit.

Wow.

Flint seemed to feel the same as me. "Saint Jabari. We don't deserve you!"

"And you don't deserve to look as good as you do in that giant sock," Jabari laughed.

In a weird way, he was right. If anyone could pull off that outfit, it was muscly Flint. But he wasn't the only one who looked awesome. There were a lot of costumes. A lot of shark stuff. A lot of people. Including Jazz and Clyde.

I wasn't sure it was Jazz Bonnie I was seeing after Flint and J left to sign in to skate, until the crowd thinned out and I was able to take in the flannel and the boots. He was holding a thick rope, and at the end of it was that awesome golden mane framing the fierce face of Clyde. Or rather, the funny face of Clyde. Jazz had found one of the shark hats and put it on Clyde's head. He still looked really noble, actually. Which goes to show how cool Clyde is. I stared at them until Jazz looked right at me. Then I smiled and waved. He did a little salute and then pointed to Clyde. I laughed out loud and gave him a thumbs-up. He smiled back and looked really happy.

"Who's that?"

Mom startled me with her question. I didn't know that she'd come up behind me. Or for how long she'd been standing there. I worked frantically to get my head straight. To create some story that would make sense. I felt a pull that was like a heavy weight. There was a part of me that wanted her to know the truth—how great those two were, how awesome it was that they had come here to support her. That really meant a lot to me. But Flint, Jabari, and I had agreed to keep our friendship with Jazz and Clyde a secret. So I made my face blank.

"Who?" I asked. A bunch of skaters busted through the place Mom was looking. When I glanced back across, Jazz and Clyde the shark dog were gone. I saw

Mom scanning the crowd, a crease across her forehead. A bunch of guys from Mission Skate were lining up to do some runs, right in front of the space where Jazz and Clyde had been. Her eyes landed on them, and her expression settled. "No one, I guess. Never mind. Pretty great turnout, don't you think?"

"It's perfect," I agreed. I looked around at the crowd again, but soldier and shark dog seemed to be gone for good.

The whirlwind of that awesome day was over the top. First, we raised more than $50,000 in just the few hours we were at Potrero. Which seemed like a lot of money to me, especially for a small school fundraiser. But it wasn't so small-school by the time it was over. It was like the best carnival and party and skate session I had ever seen all combined together.

And in the end, maybe the best part was some of the strongest skateboarding I have ever seen. Or have ever done. I was really nervous when it came time to do my stuff. I always felt great when I was on my board, but I hadn't ever skated in front of an audience. Except for Flint and J. And I never had anything really important attached to how I did. When they announced it was my turn, my heart started to race. I gripped my board and stared hard at the glowing white Oris Hart tree while kids and parents cheered around me. I wasn't sure I could do this.

But then I slid into the bowl and got that familiar feeling. I had no problem getting up enough speed to get a good snap and pop. I knew the key was going to be to go high, to do it big. You had to go high and fast if you wanted enough time to land safe and straight. I caught major air and tucked, then grabbed on while I tweaked the board toward my back. Everyone cheered and then clapped when I turned back and landed solid. I whipped around a few more times. It was amazing.

Some of the old-guard San Fran legends clapped me on the back when I finished—I found out later that they'd seen a poster about the event at Mission Skate. They wanted to help out, which blew my mind. They had agreed to help judge our tricks, but then they made everyone feel great and the crowd laugh by giving us all five stars out of five. At the very end of the event, they did some crazy stunts. It put my Crossbone to shame, but it made me just want to get better and better.

And that was probably the best thing of all. We weren't even through the first month of the year, and I was totally inspired. And, most importantly, I was on my way to nailing my New Year's resolution: help Mom beat cancer.

CHAPTER 17
HEART YARD

They say that February is the month of love. That idea used to gross me out a good bit. I'm really not into that mushy stuff. Even though I love my mom, I didn't really want to talk about it. I loved hanging out with my friends, but dudes definitely aren't into talking about that stuff. (Thank you, Jesus.) Actions speak louder than words with guys a lot of the time, and that is great by me. If I had to say what I really love, the first thing that would probably come to my mind is that I love boarding at Potrero. And at SOMA West and at Hilltop, when someone could give me a ride. I guess there are a lot of different types of love.

When the love-month of February rolled around this year, it felt different than other years. Things had changed. Obviously the most important change was with my mom. But they weren't all bad changes like you might think. This part is really hard to explain, because cancer is not a good thing. But it can lead to good things. For example, sometimes you don't have a chance to really know how people feel about you. You may not know how much people care. That is one thing that cancer did for my family. It made me really know how I felt about Mom. How I would do anything in the world for her. Like, people say stuff like that all the time—*I would do anything for my family.* But to feel that in a way that changed how you actually did things was something on a whole other level.

And then the Save-the-Shark Skateboarding Challenge. That still blows my mind. Sometimes I dream about it and then wake up and wonder if the whole thing actually was a dream. And then I remember it really happened. All of those kids and all of my teachers from school. All the money going to UCSF Medical Center and making better treatments for cancers, to help my mom and lots of other people too.

The fact that cancer was possible in the world made me want to hate the world sometimes. But the fact that the Save-the-Shark Skateboarding Challenge was possible made me love the world. That sounds cheesy as heck, but there is really no other way to say it.

So there was the cancer difference. And then there was another one. This is the first year I really thought about Valentine's Day in terms of the Valentine part. Like, *Would you be my Valentine?* Not that I thought about that constantly. But it was on the radar, so to speak. And once it was on the radar, it was hard to get it off.

It started with just wanting to thank her for what she did with Save-the-Shark. She really was one of the first ones to take the challenge and make it into something else. And when she did that, it opened the doors to a lot of people who wouldn't have been able to help otherwise. Because for sure not everyone can skateboard or wants to.

When Dori climbed the wall she was scared of and called it a Save-the-Shark, she actually created this really cool thing. That started a trend that went viral, outside of our school and even San Francisco, with folks challenging each other to do Save-the-Shark feats and give money for cancer research. Even though I was not as shocked by this thing as I would have been before the Shark Kid stuff took off, it still surprised me how these things could explode online. It was all very cool. It was nice to have surprises in life that were good ones.

I thought about going over to Inner Peaks to get her a gift certificate. Or maybe a T-shirt. Just some little thing to say thanks. But my first mistake was telling Flint and Jabari. Which seemed an obvious thing I would do because I tell them almost everything. But they went nuts over this.

"Hold up. Wait a minute. Are you serious? You're going to get Dori a present for climbing a wall? She didn't even skate! She didn't come up with the idea. She didn't have to meet with Ms. Fields a gazillion times and promise Father Russo no one would break anything!"

"She didn't humiliate herself in a blue Smurf suit," Jabari smirked.

"Exactly! Hey. Easy. You mean, rock out a super- cool Shark Man suit," Flint said.

"Yeah, Albie, seriously. Come on, man! Where's our certificates?"

I could tell they were just teasing, but they had a point. I really started to think about it. They had always done so much for me. Why was I concerned with doing something special for Dori? I didn't really have a good answer for that. She was just on my mind in a way that was different than anyone else. I couldn't really say why.

But after I had that conversation with Flint and J, things got a little weird between us. Which was a bummer because I had been feeling so up about everything before that. And then this Dori thing just messed it up a little bit. Not in a huge way, but I found out they were hanging out some without me. Which I tried not to care about. But it did hurt my feelings a little anyway.

I didn't know for sure that the problem had to do with the conversation about Dori. But that was the only thing that had been different between us. And then I tried to text them about going over to board at Potrero, and I didn't get any answer from either one. Which was kind of strange.

I decided to bag it and just go hang at Mission Skate and talk to the guys there. I wondered about doing Save-the-Shark boards and helmets. If we made them all the time and not just for a one-time fundraiser, maybe they could sell them and the money could go to UCSF. I was even thinking that maybe I could paint boards with sharks. Or sharks and trees. The idea made me really excited. I wasn't sure how all that worked. But I thought they might know.

So I slid into the shop and ran smack into Jabari. He looked really surprised to see me and then kind of guilty. I wish I could say he didn't have that look, but he clearly did. It made me sad. I knew he'd gotten my text and had just blown me off.

And he acted so weird. He practically blocked me from walking in. He jumped up and was right in my face really fast. With that strange, panicked, guilty look.

"Oh! Albert! Hey, man. What's up?" He was talking really fast.

Meanwhile there was a big crashing sound over on the counter. A bunch of stuff was hitting the floor behind it. Flint was over there, trying to catch it. But he was doing a terrible job. Honestly, he was making even more of a mess.

"Hey. Not much. Just thought about boarding some. What're you guys doing?" I tried to sound casual. I didn't want them to know how much they'd hurt my feelings. I wasn't even sure why that was so. I wasn't a baby. And they didn't have to hang with me if they didn't want to. That was fine. No problem at all.

Flint stopped "helping" at the counter and jogged over to me. "Sure! Let's do it," he said, and he and J exchanged a look. It made me feel worse. Never mind, they didn't have to change their plans to be with me.

"Actually, I have a ton of homework, I forgot. I'm just going to head back," I said. I could not wait to get out of there.

"Are you sure? What homework?" Flint looked confused. He wasn't the best at staying on top of all our assignments. Unlike Jabari, who was always on top of everything school-related. Jabari knew I was full of crap as soon as I said it. He was looking at me really closely. I made a point of not looking back.

"Yeah, no, it's cool. I have extra because I bombed that last math quiz. I'll catch you guys later."

I'd been proud of my B+ on that quiz. I'd had to work so hard for it. But that didn't matter more than leaving this scene as fast as I could.

I felt really miserable. It started to bubble up like I was feeling mad, but I shut that right down. I pictured a sleet storm pelting hard ice all around. Then the ice turned to snow. It fell like soft balls of cotton and covered everything with a smooth blanket. I took a deep breath.

Even though I had thought about doing something nice for Dori, I had not actually done anything. And even though I had basically sprinted away from Mission Skate, I still felt crappy. The next day was Valentine's Day, and I was not feeling the love.

But then I thought of Mom. I couldn't wait to get back to see her, actually. That is the thing about family. When everyone else lets you down, home is the place where you know someone has your back.

I didn't want to make a big thing of it. But I did stop in at Rite Aid and got Mom a silly card. And a red rose from a bunch they were selling out of a bucket by the registers. I didn't know if that was goofy, but they looked pretty to me. I also saw a cool leash that had a wild black-and-white design. It looked really funky, kind of artsy. But strong. When you looked closer, the black-and-white parts were actually music notes. I remembered the rope that Jazz had on Clyde at Save-the-Shark. I was really excited to get this for them. I found a cool card that just had a skateboard on it, no Valentine message. I got all of those things and a black pen so I could write my cards. I was going straight to the lot and then home. Mom was already there. I was feeling a lot better.

When I went by Jazz's camp, he wasn't there. Clyde was gone too. But the sleeping bags and their other things were still on the ground. I wrote a little message on the card and set it on top of the stuff. Then I booked it over to my house. I felt a little silly carrying a flower and a card. For my Mom. I wasn't sure if that was better or worse than having it for a real girl.

But Mom loved it. She squealed when she saw it. She hugged me until I couldn't breathe. She set my card on display on the mantle with the rose, which she put in a little vase with water.

"Albert, this is so thoughtful! How nice. This is going to make tomorrow so much better."

"Yeah, Valentines, ugh," I said and rolled my eyes.

"Well, yes. It is a little over the top, isn't it? I sure wouldn't choose to spend the day at the hospital, but whatever. Having my last treatment tomorrow is the best Valentine's gift I could get!! Woohooo! Well, the best gift besides my hilarious card and my beautiful flower." She touched my cheek and smiled.

Last round of chemo? How could I have forgotten that? Was that even right? Of course it was. Six months of medicine, and she was going to finish it all tomorrow. That meant I would be going home with Flint and spending the night at the Petersons. That was kind of a bummer. But the end of chemo was great. It was really awesome, actually.

That night, when I fell asleep I had the wildest dreams. I dreamed I was in the ocean, and sharks were swimming all around me. But they weren't scary at all. They were long and lean, protecting and pulling me. We went deep into the water, and then we busted over the top and then back down again. In my dreams I could hear the sound of the ocean, waves crashing, hissing over the sand and then pulling back out again. And then all of a sudden, I wasn't in the water—I was on these cliffs around the shore, and I was soaring on my Oris Hart board. The sound of the waves became the sound of wheels on rock and pavement and metal. I flew around everything, faster and faster on my board. My heart was racing, and the wind whipped around my face, but it felt good and free.

I opened my eyes and could still hear the sound of wheels in my head. I laid there in my bed like that for a few minutes, listening. All of a sudden, I sat up. I actually could hear the sound of wheels on pavement! I was fully awake, and I could hear them.

I pushed the covers off my bed and ran to my window. It was a little before seven o'clock, and the sun was starting to come up. There was just a little light. But enough to see a couple cars parked across from the house and maybe ten guys zipping around on boards. And something weird in the front of our house.

I strained my eyes to see and finally could make out dozens and dozens of hearts sticking out of the grass on Popsicle sticks. They were all different colors and stretched as far as I could see. Our whole yard had become a Valentine's heart yard.

Someone was bent over in the street. As he straightened up, I saw the words, "Happy Valentine's Day and Last

Chemo, Mrs. D!!" and "Congratulations, Mary!" in bright red and pink chalk. I just stood there and watched as the guys whipped around on their boards, adding the last hearts to the already-covered space. My fingers closed over my shark-tooth necklace as I watched. As it got lighter, I could make out the outlines of Flint and J among the boarders. This must have been what they were doing at Mission Skate yesterday. Wow.

I ran down the hall and into Mom's room. She was dressed and getting her shoes out of her closet. She hadn't heard anything, so she had no idea. I thought about how I had forgotten about the last treatment but my friends had not. I thought about all the guys at the skate shop. I thought of Big Anne and Dr. Pahlavi, who I knew were in their cars outside. I thought of the doctors at UCSF and the nurses at the cancer center who were waiting to help my mom that day. There were so many people who cared about us. And there was proof of it all over our yard.

My heart was pounding as I pulled Mom down the stairs. I couldn't wait for her to see what was outside. If she was feeling good about today before, she would feel amazing now. There was more than one kind of medicine, I decided. There was the kind you smeared on your knees after you crashed and burned trying a hard trick, and the kind that came in a pill you choked down and made yourself swallow. There was the kind you got out of bottles and drank even when it burned your throat. And the kind that pumped through IV tubes that were stuck in your arm as you spent the whole day and night in a hospital bed. And then there was the kind that was probably the best of all, invisible until it became paper and glue and sticks and words and busted out of the ground like a million blades of magic grass.

SPRING

CHAPTER 18
THE HATEFUL MATH OF CANCER

Mom's amazing Valentine's Day seemed like a million years ago instead of just weeks earlier after everything fell out of my book bag onto the floor, and I realized that there's a reason why I like science and I love art and I hate math.

There's an answer to everything in science. You just have to find it. You just have to ask the right questions, and then you can determine the answer. If you experiment enough, you should be able to find what you need. Art is even better. With art you can make whatever you want—if you can imagine it, you can create it. You have all of the answers and you control all of the questions, and you can turn that into something beautiful or fierce.

Math is about numbers, and numbers are hard. They mean what they mean, and it doesn't matter what you want or imagine or need. They say what they say, and you can beg or cry or rage, but one plus one will always equal two. If you need the answer to be four or five or one hundred, that is just too bad for you.

Cancer is a mathematical problem, when you come right down to it.

At the end of the day, it sure isn't about science. Don't be fooled into thinking that there is a science to chemotherapy, which is supposed to be medicine that makes the cancer go away. Chemo is so tough and so hard, it makes your whole body tired and weak. It makes your hair fall out, and it changes everything you do. When you're getting your chemo, that's all you can do. And when you're not getting your chemo, you're planning for when you are, or you are trying to get back to normal after you've had it. I thought there was a science to this medicine, that the question of Mom's disease had an answer and that science said it was this chemo, this rotten, awful, terrible chemo that was so crappy it put Mom in the hospital when she started it and then made her go back in the hospital overnight once a month for six months straight to take it.

Cancer isn't about art. Art is something awesome and solid and everything that can be imagined, like the Save-the-Shark Skateboarding Challenge, where everywhere you looked there were cool things that made you feel better. Wild T-shirts with bright patterns. Banners and signs and cards and music. Fierce boards with amazing designs. My Oris Hart board that had the most amazing design of all. Art can seem like a superpower when what you see makes you feel strong, or when it can give you hope. But it's not real. It does not translate into something real.

The hateful math of cancer comes down to numbers like CA-125. That horrible number is a number you never want to know because it means you have cancer in your body. If you do have it, then you take the science of chemo and the art of treatment and you try to get that number to move. If it moves one way, then you're golden. If it moves the other, then you're in trouble. All you can do is hope that the art and science of cancer will beat the numbers of cancer in the end.

After Mom finished her chemo in February, she had to wait a month to see what happened with the numbers of her cancer. I knew she had gone in for the test but thought it would be a few days before we would hear anything about it. So I didn't have it on my mind when she walked into the kitchen. I was doing my homework at the kitchen island, and she leaned up against it. She told me she had heard back about her CA-125 tumor marker test.

It turned out that J's mom had been able to look up the result the day before because the lab runs the test once a day. Mom told me this and said that she wanted to talk with me about it. I could see the strain on her face, and I felt my body brace. Obviously if this was totally great news, she wouldn't be starting the conversation this way. But I did not freak out. I told her sure, that was fine. She sat next to me and put her hand over my hand.

"Albert, my CA-125—you remember what that is? Right, right, sorry. Of course you do. So they did the test to check my CA-125, and honey ..." she swallowed hard and tightened her grip on my hand, then said, "the numbers have gone up."

I worked to keep my breathing steady. I knew we wanted the numbers to go the other way. So this meant that the chemo had not worked. I squeezed her hand. I thought of all that she had gone through these past months. The surgery. The hospital. Her hair. Missing her students. How hard she had fought. I couldn't believe that she had done so much, and still her sacrifices had not taken care of the problem. Thinking of her pain, I pictured our practices at school this month for the Living Stations of the Cross, all the readings and music that tell about what happened leading up to when Jesus died. It was so sad, almost too much. All the suffering. I felt really sorry about that.

But just like Easter was on the other side of the Living Stations, I felt really happy that we had a Plan B. I smiled at her and pulled my hand out from under hers. I rubbed my hands together and took a deep breath. It would be important for me to be solid for her with this next part, so I smiled big.

"I'm so sorry, Mom. I know it's been rough. It would've been great if it were all over. But now we'll just have to do the next thing. When can they start you on the Save-the-Shark medicine?"

Mom had looked confused when I started smiling, and that look just got deeper on her face while I spoke. She cleared her throat.

"I ... I don't know what you mean, sweetie," she said. "I have an appointment to go in to talk about next steps, but Save-the-Shark money? The Save-the-Shark medicine ...?" Her voice trailed off. Her forehead was creased.

I kept my smile on, but my heart was starting to beat harder in my chest. This made no sense. Was this chemo-brain? Why was she so confused? I spoke really slowly.

"You know, Mom. The Save-the-Shark Challenge, the fundraiser. We raised over $50,000 from Holy Hands alone. For new treatment options for rare and unusual cancer. So you have that medicine to try now. And I know it will work this time! This will be a much better treatment."

I spoke with confidence. But her expression still looked confused. She thought for a moment about what I had said. Then her face changed. It went through several changes, actually—a surprised look when she got it, the quickest of smiles, and then really worried. And then really sad. She took my hand again.

"Oh, Albert. Sweetie, the fundraiser was the coolest thing ever! What you kids did ..." Her voice broke, and I could tell she was working hard not to cry.

"But that money is not for me. That money doesn't go to my treatment. It goes toward research to help come up with new treatments, yes. But that process takes a really long time."

I let her words sink in. I didn't get what she was saying. All along, the Save-the-Shark fundraiser was to raise money for cancers like my mom's. For a cure. That is what we needed, and that is what we worked for.

"I don't understand. The money goes to a cure—but not one that you can use?"

"Well, I guess it may be possible down the road. But Albie, these things take time. It's definitely not an option today. I'm so sorry, sweetie."

I couldn't believe it. I just couldn't believe it. I felt actual shock, just this numbness over my body and my mind. I couldn't breathe. I couldn't think. We sat in silence for several minutes.

Then it was like something cracked open, and I snapped out of it. And I felt so stupid. What a loser—how could I have been so clueless? I had never even asked how the fundraiser would help my mom! I had just gone along thinking it was all for her, that if there was anything that went wrong with her treatment, I would've helped to fix it. I think it was so important for me to believe that good would always win in the end that I let myself believe this idea. Which was like a fairy tale you would tell a preschooler. No. It was a lie.

A lie.

All of a sudden, I just couldn't sit there anymore. I bolted up from the table and ran to my room. I tugged open my desk drawer and opened my cash box. I grabbed all the money inside and looked around for my backpack. I turned it over to dump my school stuff out—my self-portrait from art and my science book and my math test with its big red C+ all crashed onto the ground. I turned the bag back upright and shoved my money in. I threw in my helmet and a sweatshirt. I didn't know where I was going to go, but I knew I had to get out of there ASAP.

I didn't look at Mom as I stomped through the kitchen toward the back door. I grabbed my board leaning up against the back wall and pulled the door open and walked out. I could hear Mom calling me, but I did not turn around. I tucked my board under my arm and started to jog.

It felt good to run, even with the backpack and the board. It let me still feel mad. Each time my foot hit the street, it felt like I was pounding that stupid cancer.

But soon all I wanted to do was get on my board, especially when I hit 22nd Street.

I let the air hit my face as I started to go down. This street was so steep. I thought maybe it was the steepest street in San Francisco. I knew Mom didn't like me skateboarding on this kind of hill. Well, I didn't like Mom having cancer. Sometimes things happen we don't like.

I saw a police officer leaning against his car at the corner. I didn't think he would be so into my raging boarding plan. I made a sharp turn and ducked into a side street and noticed a cab parked over in front of a small grocery store, and I knew exactly where I wanted to go. I tucked my board under my arm and walked very casually up to the car. I used my best manners when talking to the cabbie, even though I wanted to scream. I told him where I was headed, and he gave a thumbs-up. I jumped in the car, and we were off.

So many bad things were crashing in my brain. I couldn't get any of my strategies to work. I pictured bright lights in a room, but when I went to turn them off, I punched the wall instead. I thought of crashing waves, but they did not turn into a soft hiss on the sand. They got bigger and bigger, a tsunami that crashed over houses and cars and animals and people. Madonna's black birds shrieked in my head, flapping and swirling around the sky until it was dark as night.

I thought of my last strategy, prayer. I laughed in an ugly way when I had my usual guilty thought that it was my last strategy and not my first. Because I was over God. Where had He been when my dad was in Iraq? Where had He been when my mom's body was growing cancer, for what was probably years, without any sign or clue? I felt so mad that I was shaking.

"Hey. You okay back there, buddy?"

The cabbie was watching me closely in his mirror, his eyes locked on mine. I could tell he was trying to figure out how old I was. Suddenly I was desperate to make it to Russian Hill. Even though I hardly ever went there, and never to skateboard. I wanted to disappear, and this was the next best thing. He could not take me back to my neighborhood.

I swallowed hard.

"Yes, sir. Great! Can't wait to meet up with my friends on Lombard."

I tried a smile. This time it didn't come easy. It felt so fake, like my face was going to break. I remembered one year when Uncle Wood's friend got Bell's palsy walking on the beach when it was crazy windy, and half of his face was paralyzed. I felt like my whole body was paralyzed like that, tight and hard. Hopefully it didn't look as bad as it felt.

"You guys are crazy to take your boards up there, if you ask me," he answered and shook his head.

He slammed on the brakes, and the car lurched forward. My board popped off the seat and crashed into the back side of the front seats of the car. It made a satisfying smacking sound as it fell. The cabbie opened his window and started yelling at the driver of a minivan who had parked and was unloading in the middle of the street. I was glad that the focus was off me. I went back to being mad at God.

But it was too strange and too bad to think about holding onto that feeling. I knew I would be really out of control if I did that, and I knew that I didn't want to be out of control. I thought of my prayer strategies again, and I imagined the sign of the cross. I felt for the wheel of my board and held it. I couldn't focus on the Creed, and my hand wandered to another wheel. I clutched it and thought, *Our Father,* and then I stopped. A lump formed in my throat. *Our Father. Father father father father.* I started to panic.

I took a deep breath and desperately tried to remember my rosary. *Hail Mary full of grace the Lord is with thee* ....

Saying Mom's name made me feel sad but calmer too. I said it again. *Hail Mary hail Mary hail Mary.* I leaned my head back on the seat. The prayer washed over me. I let it run through my mind, and I tried again to relax. *Blessed are thou among women and blessed is the fruit of thy womb Jesus. Holy Mary Mother of God pray for us sinners now and at the hour of our death ... our death our death our death....*

My head felt like it was going to explode. My strategies flew through the air like shattered glass, and I couldn't see straight. I was so mad. I was furious. I was seething like I had never seethed before.

My hand released the wheel, and I pulled out my phone. I was breathing hard and fast. I punched in my password and my home screen popped open. There were two texts from my mom on the screen, *Albert I am sorry it will be OK pls call me* and *sweetie where are you please call me*. I tapped them so they would disappear. We were way past ten minutes at this point, but I didn't care. I swiped the screen until I found what I wanted. The white bird in the blue box looked like a dove, and that made me think of church. I pushed that thought away and focused on the Twitter app Flint had downloaded for me. I stared at it and felt the slightest hesitation. But I didn't let myself really think about it. I opened the app and logged in.

Twitter opened to our Shark Kid account that Flint had set up. We used "Mission:Skate" as our password so we all would remember it when we wanted to use it, although I never did. Suddenly I wished that Flint and Jabari were with me. I needed them so badly, it felt like an actual pain in my body. I thought maybe I should text them instead of getting on Twitter. But the seething was stronger than the thinking, and so I typed my first ever tweet.

LIFE IS A SCAM

I pressed "Tweet" and watched it swoosh into the feed. I opened another new blank message, and my fingers punched the keys.

NO HOPE NO HOPE NO HOPE!!!!

Tears burned my eyes. I launched that one into the Twitterverse too.

I thought of the Save-the-Shark Skateboarding Challenge Fundraiser and how it had exploded all across social media, just like my shark rescue had. And how it was all a big fat lie. All of that hard work and all of those people. The signs and the ramps and the music and the art and the T-shirts and the donations. So much money we had raised, and for what? It made me so mad, I wanted to rip my shark-tooth necklace right off my neck. I still couldn't believe it.

Nothing we had done would help my mom. I wanted all the people to know just how stupid they were.

STUPID SHARK TOOTH WE TOOK THE TOOTH FROM A SHARK HOW DUMB IT NEEDS ITS TEETH TO LIVE SO PERFECT FOR THE TRUTH

WE MADE IT WORSE NOT BETTER

I jabbed the screen so that one would post too.

The cab had started to slow down and was making its way over to the side of the road. The cabbie looked into the mirror and was watching me closely again. I made my face seem calm and boring.

"Is this okay, son?" he asked.

"Sure, it's great," I said and pulled out a wad of money, much more than the actual cost, but I didn't care at all.

I passed the money to him and tucked my board under my arm. I opened the door and started to get out onto the sidewalk, but before I left I had one last thing to say. I looked down at the Twitter postings on my screen and typed one last thing before slamming the door so hard it made the cabbie jump.

I HATE EVERYONE

CHAPTER 19
HELP

For a kid who was famous on social media and who was known by everyone in his entire school and had thousands of followers on Twitter, it was pretty easy to disappear. Not that I couldn't be found. I just stayed in my room all the time. Miserable. Embarrassed. Lucky to have someplace to be all by myself when there was no one I wanted to see.

Mom let me have my space at first. She's always been pretty good at that, even if I'm in trouble or she needs to figure out something with me, she'll wait until I am in a decent place before we have to talk. This time I even missed school, just holed up in my room listening to music and sleeping. I felt so tired. I'd slept all night. But I just felt like I could close my eyes and sleep and sleep and never wake up. Maybe that's what I hoped for.

Mom let me have that first day. But this next morning, she came in and woke me up. I pulled the pillow over my head and turned my back to her.

"I'm not going," I mumbled through my covers.

"You are," she answered. "But you aren't going to class."

Interesting. But maybe worse. I poked my head out.

"Mom, I can't. Not after what happened. Not after Twitter. I just can't be at school."

"So your plan is to stay in your room forever? Not pass your grade? Never go to high school? I just don't really get the endgame here, Albert. I agree that was a mess. But staying in your room by yourself doesn't clean it up."

I looked at her closely. A wave of guilt washed over me. My stomach hurt. Mom had so much to deal with—of course more than me. And now I'd really messed things up. She must be so embarrassed. You'd think the least I could do was to stay out of trouble. What a jerk. Part of me just wanted to cry and crawl into her lap like when I was a little kid. Not that I could ever tell her that.

I didn't want things to get worse. I sat up in bed. I knew I was going to school. The thought made me want to puke. But where else was I going? Mom said no class. Was I in in-school suspension for the way I acted on Twitter? Could Holy Hands do that?

Holy Hands could do that, Mom told me, but they weren't going to. Instead of going straight to class, I had to go and talk to Sister about what had happened. I think I had every feeling you could think of when I heard that. Panic. Relief. Shame. Somewhere in there was hope. For the smallest second, I thought of preschool. Maybe Sister was exactly who I needed right now.

I was glad when Mom dropped me off at school early—I didn't want to see anyone as I was walking in.

As she drove away, my stomach flipped a little. I decided to skip my locker and to go the back way, just to be safe, around the gym and the foreign language trailers off the lacrosse field. I had my head down and was walking fast when I ran hard into someone busting around the corner going the opposite direction. My head jerked up in startled surprise, then happy surprise. Flint was in front of me rubbing his chest where we'd collided.

"Oh man, I'm sorry. You okay?"

Flint didn't answer me. He looked mad. Or actually, not mad, something else, like he was in pain. Had I hurt him? It didn't seem likely. Flint was like a tornado made of concrete on the football field.

"Hey. Seriously, are you okay?"

His face changed in a weird way. He closed his eyes. He nodded strangely and then cleared his throat.

"Better question, are *you* okay?"

I could feel my face starting to get hot. Here we go. Man, everyone was going to be on me about this. Of course, that was totally my fault.

But to be fair, Flint wasn't everyone. In fact, he was one of my very best friends. For the first time, I wondered why he hadn't been with the others earlier. I looked at him closely.

"I'm fine. Honestly. I shouldn't have scared everybody. I was just mad. But what's going on with you?"

Flint took a deep breath. And then he let it out. Hard. He started to cry.

I was so shocked that I didn't know what to say. This was the last thing I expected to see. Somewhere in the back of my mind it occurred to me that other people have problems too.

I put my hand on his shoulder. He let me for a second and then pulled himself out from under it. He looked at me and bit his lip.

"It's Jazz and Clyde."

Oh no. "What happened?"

Flint tilted his head back. He closed his eyes for a second.

"J and I just wanted to drop some things off for them, you know, like we sometimes do. Jabari had a bunch of food, and I had some drinks and candy and dog treats."

"Yeah, I know. I've left stuff like that for them too. But what's wrong with that? What happened?"

"Man. I just … I just don't even know, Albie. We came down the path like we always do. Except they weren't at their usual spot. They were closer to the end. So I had a Coke in my hand and I started running toward him with it. I just meant to give it to him to cool off, you know?"

This wasn't making any sense. There wasn't anything in this story that should end badly. But then I remembered Jazz clamping his hand over my mouth that day. The way he wasn't really himself. I hadn't told anyone about that, not even Flint and Jabari. I started to get a really sick feeling.

"So I run up with the Coke, and he turns around just as I'm getting to him. And … I just don't know. He starts screaming. He covers his face and falls on the ground. I step back and then I hear J saying '*run.*' And I just turn and run. And Jazz is sort of running and sort of crying. I mean, he wasn't really going after me—he would've caught me if he had wanted to. But he just kept coming my direction. And screaming." Flint swiped his eyes with the back of his hand.

"Oh man. Flint, I'm so sorry. That's awful."

"Well, it's not the worst part. All that screaming got people on us. Somebody called the cops. They came crashing into the back lot just as Jazz was coming out. J and I jumped to the side—I don't think they realized we had been back there. But they grabbed Jazz Bonnie."

I took a deep breath. As bad as the thoughts were that I had crashing in my head, I wasn't ready for the next part. The tears filled Flint's eyes again.

"Albie, they took Clyde."

It felt like someone had punched me in the stomach. No. *No!* Not Clyde. He had to be okay. I thought about Jabari wanting us to tell our parents right away. I thought about when I lied to Big Anne in the consignment shop. I thought of when Mom saw Jazz and Clyde and I could have told her all about them. But no. I was so smart, I had it all figured out. Even when I knew Jazz wasn't okay, I kept the lies going. This was all my fault.

Flint waited for me to open my eyes, but when that didn't happen, he kept talking.

"I think they called Animal Control. I went up to the officers and tried to talk to them, but they kept blowing me off. And then J checked his phone and saw your tweets. When J said we should call your mom, I was scared to do it. I thought we'd get into big trouble. But I'm glad Jabari did it anyway. Because sometimes we just need help, right?"

CHAPTER 20
READ THE COMMENTS

What Flint said to me was exactly right. I grabbed Flint's arm and dragged him over to the garden where Sister and I usually met. He didn't try to stop me. When I turned the corner, I saw that she was already there, scrolling down through something on her iPad. She looked up and saw me and jumped off the bench. I braced myself as she came charging in my direction. It looked like she was really mad at me.

But when she got in front of me, she threw her arms around me and hugged me as tight as she could. It actually hurt a little bit. Once I got over my surprise, I was happy to have that pain. It certainly wasn't what I had been expecting.

"Oh, kid," she finally said, and she stepped back, holding me in front of her at arm's length. "Albert. Are you okay?"

Her blue eyes looked very intently into mine. I swallowed.

"I'm ... I'm fine," I said, the automatic answer coming before I could think.

But this wasn't the usual deal. I couldn't really crank out an NWLWL like usual. Maybe more important, I didn't really want to. All I could think of was Jazz and Clyde. Or, that I had screwed up everything. Even just the thought of lying to Sister made me feel so bad. I cleared my throat.

"I'm not great. We have a problem, Sister. Not Twitter. Something else. We need your help."

Sister turned and noticed Flint standing next to me.

"What's going on, guys?"

And we told her. Everything. The words spilled out like a waterfall—we were gushing all over each other to tell her about our friends.

She listened very carefully. She didn't look mad or upset. When we finished, she was quiet for a minute.

"Wow, that's a lot. But I think I can find out what's going on. There're folks I can call who can let us know what's happening with Mr. Bonnie and his dog. Did they take them together?"

Flint looked miserable.

"I think Animal Control took Clyde."

Sister paused for a moment.

"Okay. The clock may be ticking there."

She saw both of our faces fall when she said that. She put her lips together. Then sighed.

"So how about this. Once Albert and I finish our talk, I'll go and make some calls. If Clyde is at Animal Control, I'll get him. He can stay with me for a little bit. We can figure this out."

I could see from Flint's face that he was as relieved as I was. This didn't solve everything, but it was a start.

"Okay. Okay! Okay, thank you, Ms. Fields," Flint said.

He threw his arms around her and gave her a huge hug. She sort of disappeared in his arms. Then he jumped back and patted her a little bit.

"Okay!" he said again and pulled on his backpack straps.

"Okay, then!" she hollered back and laughed a little.

It felt so good to hear that sound.

"Guys, after school come by my room. Or even at lunch if you want. This isn't something that should be on you, okay? There's a lot going on here. I'll figure out what's happening, and then we'll know the best way to help. Sound good?"

Flint nodded and then smiled at me. Not his usual stuff, no silly talk today. But he did look like he felt better. I know I did. At least about this. Flint took off down the sidewalk, heading back toward class. I wished I could go too. But I hadn't even started talking about my deal. That was about to change though.

"How're you feeling, Albert?" Those eyes. Bright. Wide. Safe.

"I just—I just don't know what to do now. I really messed up," I said.

Now that Clyde and Jazz Bonnie were out of my head, thoughts of my tweets pressed inside my brain. I'd worked hard to keep them out of my mind, but they refused to stay away.

"Well, you're not the first person to go on a verbal rampage on social media and on Twitter especially. But you're correct that we need to work through this. So, let's take it piece by piece."

She led me back over to the bench, and we sat down. I looked at the ground. She waited for a moment. When I didn't say anything, she spoke again.

"First, let's talk about why you were so upset."

Ugh. I really didn't want to go there. But not talking about it had clearly backfired. I sighed.

"Yeah. I was upset about Mom's tumor marker test." My voice cracked when I said that. I cleared my throat and looked straight ahead.

"And that makes total sense. It was not what we'd hoped for. And that's really hard, especially after all she has been through."

Sister shook her head. I waited for her to say, *But that's not a reason to act so crazy.* Or, *It doesn't really mean anything and we need to stay positive.* But she didn't. We just sat quietly for a minute. Then she spoke again.

"And it sounds like there was some confusion about the Save-the-Shark Challenge?"

I felt my face go hot as she said that. What an idiot I was. To think that our money would go right to Mom. Research takes a really long time. Years sometimes! I guess I had just thought what I had wanted to be true and didn't really consider anything else beyond that.

"I just wanted to do something. I just wanted to help. I thought maybe we had. But I get it. I know it takes a long time to come up with treatments and cures."

"Yeah, maybe, but I absolutely get what you were thinking though," Sister said. "It's one of the hardest things about someone you love being sick. Feeling helpless. Wanting to help. It's something that we all go through. It makes a lot of sense that you would feel that way. And actually, I have something to talk to you about later on that topic."

Sister bent her head down so she was looking at me right in the eyes.

"Here's the main thing. You know you are a blessing to your mom and always have been. You are a comfort. Just by being you. By being Albert Christian Davidson, you *are* helping. You have to know that."

Her words sounded impossible to me. I looked hard at Sister. Maybe she knew the No Worries Little White Lie trick too.

"It doesn't feel like enough," I mumbled.

"We are imperfect, and we are constantly challenged. But we are also enough. You are a child of God. Think about that, kid. What that means."

We sat quietly for a moment.

Then she added, "And you are absolutely human."

She reached out and touched my shoulder.

"But you're not alone."

"Well, you guys made that clear at Lombard," I said. I finally felt like I could mention that terrible moment. How I'd slammed out of the cab onto the crookedest street in San Francisco. How I tried to go down the hill on my board and had to turn so often, it was the opposite of my usual free feeling that I get when I'm on my board. How cars were piling up behind me and starting to honk, and I let the honking and the terrible twisting and the slow moving keep my anger boiling. But it got harder and harder. I started breathing faster until I couldn't stand it anymore. As I turned and rolled and turned and rolled, I started to yell. I hollered as loud as I could, louder than the car horns or the crazy voices in my head.

But then I heard something louder than me—my name! Someone was shouting my name. And I looked down the street and saw Mom with her arms locked into Sister's on one side and Big Anne's on the other. Dr. Pahlavi and Jabari flanked them farther down. This whole line of people, shouting for me and marching up to meet me. They looked like the people at the end of the movie *The Truman Show* when Truman tries to run away, and the whole town comes after him, marching together so he can't escape. At the time, I was furious to see them marching toward me. In fact, as far as I was concerned, MIA Flint was the only person I ever wanted to see again.

"Of course we made that clear at Lombard," Sister replied. "The second you sent those tweets, your friends were all over it. Which proves that they are real friends, by the way. Not fake friends who are just about themselves, or only about having fun. I hope you get how important it was that they went to your mom when they read what you had posted."

"I know. I do." My face burned hot again.

"Your mom called me in a bit of a panic. But I reminded her that she had you on Find My Friends. So it just made sense that we would all circle up and go. Because we all care about you, buddy. And your mom."

I let what she was saying sink in. It was pretty painful to think about what had happened. God, those tweets. Why did I have to say such crazy things? To all of those people? I wished so badly I could take it all back.

"I know. And—thank you. Thanks for talking to me even after I was a jerk on Twitter."

"Well, I think that was probably a good lesson for you. But I wouldn't worry about it too much."

"Really? Even after I said that crazy stuff to all of those people?"

"Well, I sure wouldn't do it again, although it doesn't seem like there's much of a chance of that happening. Can we agree on that much?"

I nodded hard.

"Exactly! You know, most of the ones who are following you know your deal. That's what I'm saying, Albert. There are a lot of folks out here who care about you and your mom. You aren't in this thing all by yourself."

"After my stupid tweets they probably hate me now."

"No, they don't. Have you looked at the account since you posted that stuff?"

I shook my head.

"Well, I can't believe I'm going to say this, but ... I think you should read the comments."

I raised my eyebrows in surprise. She nodded. I took out my phone and opened Twitter and went to the Shark Kid homepage. There were my tweets. I opened the last, most shameful one. There were a bunch of replies. My stomach tightened.

But then I couldn't believe what I saw. Tweets like, *Aw, Albert, hang in there! Prayers!!* and *We love you, sorry for whatever is getting you down!*

I saw more. *Shark Kid forever!* followed by *Stay Strong, Albert!* Then there was *There is* always *hope!* There were a few silly ones and a couple mean ones. But mostly it was all really good. My eyes rested on a comment that had been liked by—whoa. Twenty-one thousand people? All of a sudden, I felt a wave of panic come over me. I knew even before I looked at the pic on the side who that comment had come from. I had been down this road before, although my rescue at Lands End seemed like a million years ago.

The shame flooded back. Pope Francis had read those terrible things I'd said. But then I read what he'd replied back to me. It wasn't mean or disappointed or harsh. His tweet said, *Lord support us in this time of struggle! Let your peace be a comfort that fills our hearts and our lives.*

I read those words over and over. As I did, I felt like a weight was slowly lifting off my chest. Maybe I hadn't ruined everything.

"So, are you good for the moment?"

Sister's eyes looked really strong into mine. I nodded. She gave me a hug.

"Awesome. I'm really proud of you, buddy. Really proud. And I have something on the horizon that I think will be a cool thing. About doing something for your mom. Can you come by my room after school, and I'll run it by you? And we'll know something about Mr. Bonnie and Clyde by then."

I nodded and hugged her back. I'd never been happier to have a check-in scheduled. I still had to get through the school day though. And who knew how that might turn out. Then again, the Pope—the Pope!—was praying for me. I kept turning that over in my mind. I didn't usually pray on my own at school. But this time I said a prayer of thanks. I knew I did not deserve the second chances I had been given.

Over the next couple of weeks, Flint, Jabari, and I were crazy busy. Finally, were were able to figure out how to help Jazz, thanks to Sister. And thanks to all our parents, actually.

Everyone got in the mix in one way or another. Most important was that Dr. Pahlavi found out Jazz had seen someone to get help for something called PTSD. It was from fighting in the war, and it messed with his brain. Things that seemed normal to us could remind him of Iraq and make him scared or mad. We found out that sometimes even kids were part of the fighting that he'd seen. Flint and J and I now understood that we had triggered some of those bad memories. But now Jazz was getting some help at the Crown Hotel Shelter. And Clyde was safe with Sister.

When we did Living Stations of the Cross, I was glad to be on the crew, so I could watch. This year I really took it in. I heard people crying in the audience as they listened to the readings and songs and watched everything leading to the crucifixion. All the terrible stuff that had to happen for things to work out in the end. The worst month ever actually finished up pretty okay.

CHAPTER 21
ASIAN TEA

April brought a new focus, thanks to the idea that Sister had. She'd heard Mom talking to J's mom about some alternative things to try while she regrouped on what to do next about treatment. That's when Sister had come up with her idea. But it would take the work of our entire science class and would turn our annual field trip into a mission.

Every year the Holy Hands students go on a field trip to learn about an interesting part of the city. This year it was Chinatown, which Sister decided was quite fortuitous (one of our bonus vocab words!). Our field trip group was made up of the science and the social studies classes, and that gave her a cool idea.

Dr. Pahlavi explained to Mom about this complicated Asian tea medicine that might be another treatment for her cancer. There were really unusual ingredients in it. Everything in the tea had to be fresh. And you had to make it a certain way. You had to boil certain parts and dry others out in the sun. You had to wash some of it really carefully and put it together in a certain order. It was really hard to make. But Dr. Pahlavi actually knew a couple folks whose cancer had gotten smaller when they had used the tea. That was what Mom and Dr. Pahlavi and Sister had been talking about when Sister suddenly put all these different pieces together.

She had wondered what would happen if the science class took this on. Since we were studying the properties of matter and the periodic table of elements and chemical changes, maybe all of this could apply to this special Asian tea. Maybe my class could study all this stuff about the science behind the tea. And maybe we could make the tea as a class.

All of this got the thumbs-up from everyone. The lesson plans were approved. The kids were on board. Which made me feel pretty great. It still surprised me that people would be willing to help, but maybe I shouldn't have been so surprised. I reminded myself, *Just think of what everyone did with Save-the-Shark.* I might have thought that they had used up their energy to help with that huge event. But it hadn't been a one-time thing. It seemed like the more people did, the more they wanted to do.

Like when I walked through the halls after my first post-Twit Sister check-in and was so worried as I approached the other groups of kids around. Of course, they all knew about the Twitter disaster. But when I walked up, no one did anything mean. Lots of folks waved or said hi. Dori Martin lifted up her shark-tooth necklace and held it out in my direction and smiled. Everything was okay.

So it was a go to study the science of tea and to make this tea. After it was made, we would give it to my mom. The hardest part was going to be getting all the wild ingredients. And that's where Sister's idea came in. We could find everything we needed when we were on our field trip to Chinatown. Sister even sweetened the deal—the first team to get back to the bus with all the ingredients would get Starbucks gift cards.

"Which I know you will use for the incredible health benefits of green tea or black tea, especially after all that you will have learned about tea by then—and not for double chocolate iced cappuccinos with whip and sprinkles," she said, while everyone in class laughed.

When we got to Chinatown, everyone started straining to get out of their seats and see. It's not like we had never been there before. But not all together. And not for this reason.

I was especially happy to get to be on a team with Flint and J. This was a cancer card advantage, which sounds terrible to say. But it was something that Mom and I had noticed, and finally she came up with a phrase to describe it. Like when she first got sick and we ate all of those great dinners, better than anything we normally had. Or my being forgiven on Twitter. By Pope Francis. Or getting to be in a scavenger hunt group with my best friends. These things probably wouldn't have ever happened except for the cancer part. Was it better than not having cancer? For sure, no. Still, we were happy to take all the good stuff that came our way in spite of the bad stuff.

The night before the field trip, I looked over the items we were supposed to find.

> *Amaranth*
> *White radish root*
> *Burdock root*
> *Shiitake mushrooms*
> *Radish leaves from adult daikon*
> *Karela*
> *Wu brown rice*

Getting the stuff would be the first challenge. But then we had to handle it just right. This is where the science came in. Our groups had studied the different parts of how this Asian tea was made, and we all were becoming experts in what to do next and why. But first we had to get our hands on these special roots and vegetables and rice.

Flint was raring to get to it as soon as we jumped off the bus. Passing through the green Chinatown gate with dragons across the top got us all pumped, and everyone was excited for our search. Sister reminded us of our rules, and we took off. Each street had an adult chaperone waiting for us, so I knew we could get help if we went too far off our plan.

It was very cool just walking around. You could see fierce swords and painted masks through the glass windows of the stores on Grant Street. Wild smells came from open doorways as we passed them. I had been to Chinatown bunches of times but usually only to eat dim sum at Great Eastern, which was a restaurant that Mom loved.

Speaking of Mom, I saw we would get extra points if we stopped at St. Mary's Cathedral, even though there weren't any ingredients there. The name seemed like a good omen. And I thought about Pope Francis's tweet to me. Even though Flint thought we should head down to Clay Street and try to beat the crowd, he agreed to let us head to California Street and the cathedral instead. It was two against one for the cathedral plan—me, because I thought of Mom, Jabari because he would never give up a chance to get extra credit.

The cathedral was pretty cool. It was the first Catholic cathedral in the city and built from granite from China. It was not the first time I realized how so many of us were connected in some kind of way. I thought about how the magic of China had created this church that had survived since the 1800s. I prayed that the magic would carry over to the special Asian tea, and I lit a candle. Then we were off.

There were a lot of interesting things to see. The balconies on one street were all painted crazy-cool colors. I took a picture of them with my phone. I liked how they had such interesting designs and ran across all the buildings, linking one to the other.

With all of the sights around us, and with our easily distracted tour director, Mr. Bojangles, we could have fallen down a rabbit hole like Alice in Wonderland. But we didn't blaze a trail, really. There was enough good stuff to see just following along with our scavenger hunt directions.

The other groups had our same destinations but in a different order. It was fun to pass them coming in as we were going out. It felt good that we were getting these things for Mom. Except at first, we couldn't find the burdock root. Which seemed crazy since there were so many markets on Stockton Street. I felt a little bit panicky—what if no one could find this ingredient?

But then Jabari talked with a nice older woman who was shaking an eggplant over a bin in the market, and she walked us around all of the overflowing boxes until we came upon it. We used our prepaid card and added it to our supply bag. Later I saw a group with a bag from Nan Hai Corporation, which wasn't on our original list of stops. I guessed they'd made a detour to make sure they had all the ingredients. The thought made me kind of mad at first, like they had cheated. But then it made me smile. Beg, borrow, lie, cheat, or steal ... in this case I was for it.

After we finished getting all of our stuff, our last stop was Ross Alley Fortune Cookie Company. The smell was so delicious. It was pretty neat how fortune cookies get made. We all got to sample the cookie wafer and then take one with a fortune for the road.

As we walked back toward the bus, we munched on our cookies, and Flint pulled out his fortune. He shook his head as he read it.

"Do what?" he said. "Seriously, what the heck does this mean?"

Jabari looked over his shoulder. "What's the problem?"

"I don't understand my fortune is the problem! What does that mean? It can't be good."

"Well, what is it?"

Flint cleared his throat. "Ahem. Check it out. 'Two days from now, tomorrow will be yesterday.' What the heck?"

"What's not to get?"

"Are you serious, G.I.? What's *to* get? What does that have to do with all the fame and fortune that is coming my way any minute? What about my fabulous football career? Tomorrow being yesterday is just giving me a headache."

"Well, mine's a little weird too," Jabari said. He pulled out the sliver of white paper and read, "You will find a thing. It may be important."

"Whaaaat??! Somebody is dipping in the soy sauce at the cookie factory! I mean, really. *A thing?* May be important? I think the fortune guy is messing with us."

"At least he didn't put something really awful in there. 'You are a big loser.' 'Don't even think about it.' 'You are allergic to Chinese food.'"

J started laughing.

"Dude, seriously! Terrible. Oh well. At least we get a treat for our trouble."

I waited until I got on the bus to open mine. I didn't know if it was a good fortune or a bad one when I first read it. In fact, I wondered if it wasn't a fortune at all but instead a history recap plus a wacky riddle. But only if you thought of a journey as being long in stuff happening, instead of in miles. After I read it a few times, I decided it sounded pretty cool.

You will journey far for what you desire.
Your destination will reveal what you require.

CHAPTER 22
FIGHT FOR TIME NOW

Something unexpected happened when Mom stopped her chemo.

It was hard to know what it meant, because the tumor marker test had not been good. We'd wanted the numbers to go down, but they'd gone up. That meant that the chemo had not done its job. The cancer was still there.

So while Mom looked into Sloan Kettering or MD Anderson or some other big medical centers with lots more treatments, she was just off the chemo routine. And a pretty cool thing happened.

She had a lot more energy. She looked really great. She felt a lot stronger. That was the thing about chemo. The medicine worked so hard to fight the cancer that it beat the rest of her up too. Once that tough medicine stopped, she seemed to be a lot like the mom before cancer.

Except that she was changed. This was mostly a good thing. She was just happy a lot of the time. She wanted to do things and really got into them. After the Save-the-Shark event, she got into skateboarding. I wasn't sure how I felt about that, especially when she showed up at Mission Skate with cookies and brownies for the crew there to say thank you for everything they'd done. Boarders can be a sorta rough bunch. But they loved the treats.

"Yo, that's really awesome, Mrs. D," they had said. They were polite and nice.

So it worked out pretty well that Mom wanted to check out the parks. She drove me and Flint and Jabari to Hilltop and watched us at SOMA West and at her favorite, Potrero. It was great seeing her out and about and feeling good.

One day, though, she was feeling really anxious. She called J's mom in a panic, who came over and tried to calm her down. I heard them talking back and forth for a few minutes from my bedroom. Mom's voice was going up and down. She was talking really fast. I got up from my desk and walked into the kitchen where they were talking. I slid into my seat at the table and listened.

"Okay, I understand that you think we need to move faster, but you have an appointment at Sloan as soon as school gets out. What is it that you think you need to do before then? Are you having trouble tolerating the tea?"

"No. The tea has been great. It feels good to be doing something, and it is something I can do every day. I had a little rash at first, but it wasn't a big deal. The tea is fine."

"Then are you having symptoms? Pain? Are you experiencing changes that have you worried?"

Mom was quiet and stared out the window for a minute. Finally she said, "I just feel like I should be fighting."

Dr. Pahlavi reached over and held her hand. She had really long, thick hair, and it was wound into a knot at her neck. She was so smart and so pretty. I'd never really noticed how pretty she was until I saw her hold my mom's hand that way.

"You *are* fighting. You are fighting for time *now*. Giving your body a break allows you to be here, I mean really be here. Be available to Albert. Have energy for the things you love. Do you understand? You have spent the past six months fighting for time later, and that's an important thing and something I believe wholeheartedly will pay off for you. But that fight came at a price. It cost you time now. And the time now is just as valuable. It's just as worthy."

Mom breathed in really deeply. She nodded slowly like the words were making sense. I wondered if she was thinking about the things I was, like going to the skate parks and hanging out and having fun. She finally smiled.

"Thank you, Kay," she said.

She sounded much better. I was so glad. I really liked what Dr. Pahlavi had said too.

The next day, Mom came busting into my room while I was working on my math homework.

"Albert. Sorry to interrupt, sweetie. But I have a question for you. What would you think about taking a trip? You would have to miss some school."

"Sweet! I'm in. Where're we going? Charleston?"

"No. But maybe your uncle can come with us. Here's the thing. I want to go on a pilgrimage."

"A what? But where would we go for that?"

"Okay. This is going to sound bizarre. But I just read something, and I have this feeling. Check this out."

Mom passed me a little paperback book from the Loyola Press series that we have at school. I have one with all of the main Catholic prayers in it. This one was about saints. It was opened to the page about Saint Peregrine. He's the patron saint for people who have cancer. There were special prayers you could pray to him for healing.

"Um, okay, this is pretty cool. But you didn't say exactly where we would go."

Mom looked really excited. "Albert, look at his saint day."

I read down and saw that it was the fourth of May. I looked back up at Mom really quickly. That was her birthday.

"The Pope holds his special audiences on Wednesdays. May fourth is on a Wednesday. It's the feast of Saint Peregrine, and it's my birthday."

She took my hands into hers and squeezed them. She looked at me, and her eyes were bright and her smile was so wide.

"I think we should go to Rome," she whispered.

CHAPTER 23
PILGRIMAGE

That's when the whole thing blew wide open. To get to Rome that fast would mean getting plane tickets that would cost over a thousand dollars each. It seemed impossible. That is, until I told the guys what Mom was thinking.

"We just don't know about getting money for the trip," I said to Flint and Jabari.

J nodded like he got it, but Flint shook his head.

"Raise it!" he hollered, grabbing Big Anne's laptop out of her huge purse on the kitchen counter.

"What do you mean? We don't have time to do a fundraiser for this."

"That's why you are going to do the whole thing online. Ever heard of GoFundMe?"

"Maybe. Yeah, I guess."

"Dude. You are the Shark Kid. You have had tweets liked by the Pope. Do you really think folks won't give money to get you guys there?"

Suddenly I thought of all of those followers on Twitter, all of those likes. All of those replies and re-tweets. They had seemed like something not quite real, something that just existed in the air. But what if that could turn into a real way to get Mom's pilgrimage to Rome? I thought about how all of that had come to be when I saved the shark near Lands End. And Pope Francis had retweeted that tweet. And then so many people knew about me and about Mom. Maybe this was why all of that had happened.

We couldn't get to Mom fast enough. When we came busting into our house, Mom was in the front room talking to Sister.

"Whoa, where's the fire, monkeys?" Sister cackled as we came crashing in.

"We need to talk to Mom! About Rome!"

"Well, join the party. I was just talking to your mom about Rome. You know I actually have some connections here."

Sister turned back to Mom.

"My uncle is a Jesuit priest. He's a director at the Pontifical North American College, in charge of theoretical studies. He absolutely can get you and your mom into one of the audiences."

"But it has to be on May fourth. It has to be that day!"

"I'm working on that part. You know that's coming up really soon ... so I don't know. But there's a good chance."

"Well, we've been working too. Flint has a great idea for getting the money for the trip. But we wanted to make sure we could do it."

Flint launched into his idea about GoFundMe. Mom and Sister listened really closely. Flint ended up calling his dad at Wells to ask about some of the specifics. And Mr. Peterson came over with Big Anne after he got off work to set it up with Mom. This thing was really going to happen.

We set up the GoFundMe as a personal campaign and used it to tell Mom's story. We talked about our family and my dad and Iraq. We talked about Mom's cancer. We talked about Holy Hands and Save-the-Shark and all that we had done here in San Francisco. We talked about the end of chemo and the Asian tea and fighting for time now and fighting for time later. We talked about Saint Peregrine and Mom's birthday, and we talked about Pope Francis. We put it all into our GoFundMe page, and then we shared it on every social media platform we had any connection to.

And then we went to bed.

When we woke up the next day, we couldn't believe it. There was already $25,000 raised for our cause. And the number was ticking up by the minute.

"What the what?" Mom shouted when she saw it. "Albert, check this out!"

As I looked at our page, my phone started buzzing. Flint and J were texting me the coolest emojis and gifs. Mom and I danced around the kitchen and laughed. So far, this pilgrimage idea was working out great.

I had the hardest time concentrating at school that day. I watched the minutes tick off the clock so slowly. Finally, it was time to go. Everyone was meeting back at our house to figure out what to do.

When Flint and J and I walked in, all the parents were already there. They were talking and laughing and had notepads out and drinks and snacks. Everyone seemed to be getting more and more excited. It made me think of when you're bodysurfing and you paddle until you come to the best wave, that is swelling in the ocean, getting bigger and bigger and gathering more and more energy. You know when it crests and falls, it will be so freaking strong. You know it will push you hard and fast all the way to the shore.

All the adults were blown away by the response of our GoFundMe request. Given how much money had come in, my mom came up with an idea, and it changed our campaign a bit—to include a Peregrine Posse that would make the trek with Mom and me. That meant Uncle Wood would go. And Flint and Big Anne and Jabari and Dr. Pahlavi. And our travel guide and Vatican connection, Sister.

When we heard that, we whooped it up like we had won the lottery. Which we really had.

We had so much energy, we had to go outside and burn some of it off. Flint, Jabari, and I headed out with our boards and just cruised around the Castro for a bit.

"Holy smokes, dude, can you believe it?" Flint was smiling from ear to ear.

"I wonder if we'll have to make up all our missed work," Jabari said.

Flint did a heel flip and doubled back until he ran Jabari off the road.

"Please do not make me seriously hurt you," he said.

"Okay! Okay! It's not that I care if we have to or not. Just asking. Geez."

"Well, you better let that stuff go and start packing!"

We all started laughing and high-fiving. I felt like I was in a dream.

Over the next few days, we got our plan organized. We would fly to Charlotte, North Carolina, where we would have a layover and meet up with Uncle Wood. Then we would all fly over to Rome. That flight would take almost ten hours. It was hard to imagine that. At least it would happen overnight. Then with the time change, we would get there in the morning Rome time. We would have a day to explore, and then the next morning would be Mom's birthday and the audience with Pope Francis.

And everything went off without a hitch. I thought I would be so tired, but I felt like I had been shocked by an electrical socket. I had so much energy. Even after we flew to Charlotte and had to wait in the airport, I was really jazzed up. As we walked through the busy space, we came across a huge line of white rocking chairs. Flint made a big show of falling into one and rocking it dramatically.

"Ah! Yes. The king is back on his throne at last," he said in his most exaggerated Southern accent.

Big Anne grabbed the back of his chair as he rocked and caught him midway through. "Burger King, maybe. Speaking of, are you hungry?"

Flint whooped it up at the mention of food and jumped out of the chair. He took off with Big Anne down to the food court. Most everyone wanted to get something to eat since the airplane food wasn't always the greatest. I decided to stay put and to check on our Twitter feed.

So many people on Twitter were sharing prayers for healing for Mom to say when we had our time with Pope Francis. They were very cool. I showed them to her as she rocked next to me, and we favorited the ones she liked. I told her I could copy those down while we were on the plane later. If ever a prayer for healing was going to work, this had to be the time.

"These are pretty amazing," Mom said, scrolling through the list. "We'll have to figure out exactly the right thing. We won't have that much time, you know."

"Yeah. At least there are so many that are so good," I said. Once again I was amazed that people who didn't even know us would take the time to try to help us. "You just decide which one you want. We can read it together when it's time."

"It's going to be so great, Albie," Mom said and squeezed my hand.

Finally, we were able to board our last flight. Since we were flying through the night, the lights on the plane were turned down really low. It was dark and quiet. We had traded around seats, and Jabari was next to me at first, but then he switched back so he could watch a movie with his mom. I could hear Mom and Uncle Wood jabbering a couple of rows over. Sister slid into the empty seat beside me.

"Hey, buddy. Checking in," she winked. I thought of our other check-ins. Who would have ever imagined that we'd have one a gazillion miles in the air? On the way to Rome?

"I'm doing great, thank you," I whispered. "But it feels a little like a dream."

"I know, kid," Sister said. "You're right about that. But it's such a good lesson, isn't it?"

She pulled the thin airplane blanket around her.

"When you think of how bad things were feeling just a short time ago ... we could've never imagined this moment. Yet here we are. The hard times come. They just do. But they don't last. You just have to hang in there. And you have! I'm so proud of you!"

I could see her wide blue eyes glowing in the dark. I blushed.

"Thanks. For all of it. For helping to make this happen."

I felt such a rush then. For practically my whole life, Sister had always had my back.

"My pleasure, Albert," she said. I could feel her smiling in the dark.

I turned my head to the window and closed my eyes.

CHAPTER 24

WHEN IN ROME

When I opened my eyes, we were getting ready to land. Once off the plane, we grabbed our stuff and then jumped into the taxis that Sister's uncle had arranged. The drivers were very cool and wanted to show us around some, once we were in the city. My body was so tired, but I was really pumped too. I could tell right away that I loved everything about Rome. I felt the busyness of the city was kind of like San Francisco with people bustling about everywhere. But there was a different feel to this place. There was so much that was so old but also stuff that was modern and new. We passed a McDonald's that sat next to an old column. On the column was a painting that looked like it was a million years old.

I took a ton of pictures with my phone. The buildings were cream and yellow, so light compared to the gray-black squares that covered the streets. Uncle Wood said they were called cobblestones and were made of volcanic rock. The sky was the brightest blue. We passed doorways that were interesting—some were massive and dark, like they belonged on a mansion, and others were lean and brightly colored.

And the food! It was torture to see so many outdoor cafés where the food smelled so good. I ate a piece of pizza that melted in my mouth like nothing I'd ever tasted, even though I've had a million slices of pizza in my life. It was made of the thinnest crust that was almost like a cracker, covered with anchovies and something called a zucchini flower, which I was happy to see didn't look like the blooming rose I had pictured. We watched a lady in the window of the gelato store chopping tons of fresh fruit that went into the ice cream, piles of orange and strawberry. Flint ate so much that he started to look a little green. I couldn't blame him though. It was all so good.

Uncle Wood was literally spinning in circles at one point, trying to decide which direction to go since we didn't have a lot of time before our big day. He'd been teaching us about some of the art we could see in Rome, which he said was some of the best art in the whole world. We knew we were going to see some pretty cool stuff once we got to the Vatican. We'd already seen a lot of neat things just coming into the city from the airport. Our drivers brought us to the Spanish Steps, which looked kind of familiar to me. My driver told me they were built in the 1700s and have been featured in a ton of books and movies—so maybe I *had* seen them before. To celebrate the anniversary of the founding of Rome— the birthday, that is—the Spanish Steps had been covered with hundreds and hundreds of pink flowers. It looked so awesome. Flint asked how old Rome was, and Sister told us it was twenty-eight centuries old.

"*Dang!*" Flint said, and we all laughed.

I took Mom's picture in front of some of the flowers. It felt like maybe they were there just for her. It seemed like a good sign.

Full and happy, we finally settled in at our Italian home base. We were all staying at the North American Pontifical College thanks to Sister's uncle, and it was amazing. There was even a place to kick a soccer ball and to shoot hoops. Flint and Jabari decided to hang around and work out. We all seemed a little lost without our boards, which we had all wanted to bring and had all gotten shut down. I wasn't sure if I wanted to hang out at the college or go lie down like Mom or go explore or what. But just then Uncle Wood came around the corner and flagged me down.

"Oh, Albert! I'm so glad you're here. I wanted to take a walk, if you're up for it."

"Yes! Great," I said, relieved that someone else had made the decision for me.

We made our way along the Via Garibaldi, which Uncle Wood had marked on his map, over to a place called Janiculum Hill. These streets were paved just like the ones in San Francisco. That wasn't the only thing that looked like San Fran: they were pretty steep, and they curved around. Too bad we weren't boarding on this trip. I could've used some wheels to ease the climb. Uncle Wood was panting a little beside me, and sweat beaded on his forehead.

We finally got to the top of the street, and I saw a huge bronze statue of a man on a horse. It was on a massive marble base. He looked out over the city, and, following his gaze, I saw the coolest view of Rome.

"This is a monument to Giuseppe Garibaldi," Uncle Wood said. "He was a patriot and soldier who fought to unify Italy."

"I like that he's looking out over the city," I replied.

I stared at the rooftops and the cathedral domes and all the amazing shapes and colors of Rome. This had to be the best place to see all of those great sights. No wonder Uncle Wood wanted to bring me here.

"Yes, well. There's maybe a little controversy about that." Uncle Wood chuckled. "Facing this way, he has his back to the Vatican. And, more pointedly, so does his horse's big rear end. But I like your focus on what he's looking toward."

There were some trucks selling food and drinks off to the side. Uncle Wood got me a lemon soda and a package of cookies. I munched on them as we started to go back. But as I turned to go across the street the way that we came, Uncle Wood stopped me.

"This way, Albert," he said, turning down a side path. "We haven't reached our final destination yet."

I was very curious then. What could be better than the best view ever of Rome?

We made our way down a small path through a park that had several busts. It seemed very typical of this city to have little statues in a regular park—I thought of Dolores Park with its hills and tennis courts, but nothing that seemed ancient. Uncle Wood said these statues were all of guys who had helped protect Rome, who had been heroes. It smelled super nice here, like bunches of flowers.

This was another cool spot, but not our endpoint, apparently. Uncle Wood walked purposefully down the narrow path. Then he stopped.

I looked around for another massive statue or for another incredible view. But all I saw were normal steps leading down to a busy street. This seemed to be our stop, except I couldn't tell why.

"Tasso's Oak," Uncle Wood said and turned me slightly so I could see.

What was I looking at?

It was a tree. But not exactly a tree—or at least, not one that was completely there. It was kind of a thick skeleton of a tree, held up by metal props.

"The poet Tasso used to sit under this tree and write in the 1500s," Uncle Wood said. "The tree was his special place. It offered him shade and protection and inspiration."

I stood very still. I thought of my dad and his tree, which was the opposite of this broken deal. Even if it was pretty battered, though, there was something very cool about looking at a tree that had been here for all those years.

"It's been struck by lightning. It's been set on fire. All of nature and life has beaten it down. But some part of it still calls to people. It still inspires. You know, it's pretty wild to think that folks still care about this one tree. That they've put memorial bricks around it. They're propping it up with metal sticks. It may never be what it once was physically. But I'd say the spirit of this tree just keeps getting bigger and stronger. I mean, think about it!"

Uncle Wood grabbed my shoulders and looked at me. "Tasso wrote poems here hundreds of years ago! And we're here today! It's just awesome. Don't you think?"

I looked at the twisted Tasso tree, and I felt a warmth burn in my chest. I knew all about things getting bigger and stronger, even when they were so small in the world they were invisible to most people. I knew all about the magic of trees. I felt that solid feeling that comes when I am connected to my dad.

"Now, here's the best part," Uncle Wood said.

He took out his phone and snapped a picture of the Tasso tree. Then he played with the editing some: he made the picture black and white. Then he used some kind of art app that made parts of it extend and change. The Tasso tree became longer and taller, then fuller and white and glowing at the top. I gasped when I saw it. And recognized it.

Uncle Wood's Tasso tree was the Oris Hart tree on my board.

He laughed when he saw my face. "Pretty amazing, right?"

"Yes!" I said, and Uncle Wood laughed again.

"It was just something that came to me when I was looking at a photo of the sights on this hill. And I couldn't wait to show you. Full-circle moment," he said and smiled.

CHAPTER 25
MIRACLE

The next morning, everyone but me and Mom and Sister and Father Fields had to get up really early to make sure they could get in to the American section of Saint Peter's Square. They needed to be up front so they could see us and we could see them. Since Mass started at ten, they would have to be there by six to get in and be in the right spot. We had our special tickets to have the blessing with the Pope, and so we didn't have to go until nine or so. I had slept so hard after I got back from Janiculum Hill with Uncle Wood, I felt like I could sleep for a week.

But once I woke up, I was ready to get there as fast as we could go. Our pilgrimage day was here! When I saw Mom, I gave her the biggest hug.

"Happy Birthday!" I said, proud that I had remembered to tell her right away.

She smiled and gave me a kiss. There wasn't time to celebrate though—we had to get ready. There would be time for celebrations later. And there would be a lot to celebrate.

As we made our way to the Vatican, I started to feel really excited. It felt like my body was on fire, but in a good way. A powerful way. I wanted to remember every part of every second of that day.

When we got to Saint Peter's Square, I could hardly take it all in. It was so huge. All around the tops of the buildings that bordered it I saw the statues of the saints. I wondered which one was Saint Peregrine. They all looked very cool. I had the feeling they would be helping us that day. The square itself was massive. I had never seen anything so big and with so many people. They were spilling in from the entryway. So many folks, and they just kept coming and coming. It was nuts.

We all filed in where we were supposed to be. On the right of where the Pope would come, all the important religious people had their spots. Sister and Father Fields were over there. Then there were the people with medical issues, like Mom and me. There were a bunch of children who were there for special blessings. And there were a bunch of couples who had gotten married, all dressed in their wedding gowns and tuxedos, and all sitting in our special section waiting for their turn.

You could feel the excitement in the square as it filled up with even more people and as everyone waited for Pope Francis. Finally, we heard a gasp in the crowd and murmurings. Someone had seen his curtains move. He was coming!

He made his way down the steps, with the Swiss military guard around him. Everyone was going crazy.

He got to his red velvet chair that had gold rimmed all around it. He sat down and started welcoming the crowd.

Everyone started yelling and cheering. People were crying. When he welcomed them, Pope Francis went through ten or twelve different languages, saying his greetings. It was amazing. I looked out and saw Flint and J right at the front of the ropes like we had planned. I could see them cheering and waving. The greetings were very solid. Especially when he got to this one country, and all of a sudden everyone in that section started singing their national anthem. Pope Francis had to stop while they were waving flags and singing and cheering and crying. It wasn't even my country, but I was cheering, too. Mom reached over and held my hand. It was the coolest thing I had ever seen.

The Jumbotrons all around helped everyone to see the Pope's face up close. I loved looking at him in front of me and on the big screen. He had the kindest face I had ever seen. He was saying some things in English but a lot in Italian too. I felt like I could understand what it meant even though I didn't know the words. It was like the whole place was filled with magic.

Just like I had hoped it would be.

Then it was time for us to go get our blessing. We lined up with the other people in our section. I could see the kids before us, some of them taking his hand. Some kissed his ring as he blessed them. This was our chance. We had made this pilgrimage, and it was Saint Peregrine the Patron Saint of Cancer Survivors Day, and it was Mom's birthday, and I was ready to say the prayers for her healing. I looked at her and smiled and raised my eyebrows and nodded so she would know I was ready.

This was it.

Mom held my hands. There were tears streaming down her face. As we inched closer and closer to the Pope, she closed her eyes and bowed her head. She pulled out a small paper. And she began to read,

> *Make a Joyful Noise to the Lord, all the earth*
> *Worship the Lord with gladness*
> *Come into his presence with singing*

I jerked my hand out of hers, and my head popped up. What was this? This was not any one of the prayers to Saint Peregrine that we'd found! This was not any of the special prayers for healing that we'd gotten. What was she doing? This was her chance for healing, and what was she saying?

She took my hand as we moved closer. She whispered into my ear,

> *Know that the Lord is God*
> *It is He that made us, and we are His;*
> *We are His people and the sheep of His pasture.*

I started to panic. If there was ever a day to be solid and hold it together, today was the day. This was our chance for a miracle. All Mom had to do was say any of the prayers that we'd saved to cure her cancer. And we had a ton of them! All over Twitter, people had been posting things—she didn't have to come up with anything on her own.

The line was moving closer and closer to Pope Francis.

"Mom?" I tried to keep my voice steady. "Let's stick with the plan. Do you need me to get the right prayer for you?"

She slowed down and put her arm around me. She squeezed my shoulder. "I am saying the right thing."

This made no sense. I jerked out from under her. I was having a hard time catching my breath. The people behind us craned their necks around to see what was going on. We were going to have to move—soon. Why was she doing this? She couldn't mess this up.

"No!" I surprised myself with how loud I was. The noise of the square drowned it out, but not completely. Mom definitely heard me.

"Albert. Please."

"Please what? Please be okay with you not asking for what we came here for? Why are we here? What are we doing here?" I was shouting. I was just feet away from Pope Francis, and I was shouting.

"Albert, calm down. It's going to be okay."

And then it hit me like a face plant on concrete. All the times I had said whatever I had to so things would be okay. All of the times I had lied. I was a liar. Maybe God punished me for lying when Mom's tumor marker test was bad and when the Save-the-Shark money wouldn't help her. Maybe He wasn't done punishing me yet. Maybe my worst punishment was that now, *Mom* was lying to *me*. It was not okay. I felt like I was going to be sick. I looked at her right in the eyes, pleading.

"Then do what you can to make it okay! Please! Please don't give up, Mom." I stopped and took a deep breath. "Please."

My eyes filled with tears. "I can't lose you."

Something changed in her eyes when I said that. But I couldn't stop myself. I grabbed her hand and held it tight.

"I don't want you to die."

I had said it. My awful words hung between us.

Mom took my other hand. She faced me.

"Albert. You will never lose me. I will always be with you, son. Always. No matter what happens. You and me? We're bigger than Twitter and GoFundMe campaigns. We're bigger than chemo. We are bigger than cancer."

She squeezed my hands lightly. "They say God is love. Love is stronger than all of this. *All of it.*"

She looked straight into my eyes. "Do you believe me?"

I could feel my panic give way to something else. I heard the people cheering and singing. I heard my mom's soft voice. I saw Pope Francis, getting closer and closer. I looked up, and I saw his face on the big screen. I saw all of the saints surrounding us. I knew Tasso's tree was looking down at us from Janiculum Hill.

And I felt something break open in me then. I started to cry. I held on to my mom, and I cried for what she was doing. I understood this prayer. It was not one for healing. It was a prayer of thanks.

When Mom had the chance to say anything to God, after her months of sickness and her pilgrimage and her birthday, this is what she said.

Enter His gates with thanksgiving,
And His courts with praise
Give thanks to Him, bless His name
For the Lord is good;
His steadfast love endures forever.

And then we were right in front of Pope Francis. His eyes were so kind. He made the sign of the cross over Mom, and he touched my cheek.

As we moved away, I let the tears fall, and I held onto Mom. She kept saying *I love you, Albie. I love you so much. I'm so grateful for my life. This beautiful life. All I can see are my blessings. So, so many blessings.*

And I thought about Saint Peregrine and the Peregrine Posse and Pope Francis. I thought about God. And I knew that our prayers had been answered.

CHAPTER 26

HOME

I looked across the seats at Mom. We both had aisle seats so we would have more room for the long flight, but we were still across the aisle from each other. Her face was flushed and full. She had always worn her blond hair short, and now it almost looked like it had before she was sick. She had her headphones in and was humming along with her music, smiling. She looked so happy.

I was so glad to have been able to go to Italy with her on her special birthday pilgrimage. I couldn't believe that Flint and J and their moms and Sister and Uncle Wood had been able to go too. I kept playing back all the scenes of the trip like a movie in my head. Some parts made me feel really emotional. I didn't try to shut it down. I could have the feelings and be solid too.

I looked at the back of Jabari's and Flint's heads a few rows up, watching a movie together on J's iPad. I realized that soon it would be summer, and we would be able to hang out together a bunch again. That was kind of crazy to think about. It seemed like just yesterday it had been summer. I remembered when it was my birthday and I had gotten my new Oris Hart board from Uncle Wood. It had felt like the coolest thing that ever happened to me. So much had happened since then.

I thought about the GoFundMe campaign. It had exploded so much that we were going to have to decide what to do with all the extra money. Maybe donate it to UCSF. Maybe make Save-the-Shark skateboards and helmets. There were a lot of good things we could do.

This year was incredible. Awful and good. I thought about how, when it came right down to it, in that special moment in the middle of Saint Peter's Square, all Mom had in her heart to give were prayers of thanks.

She caught me staring at her and pulled her headphones out of her ears.

"How're you doing, babe?" she asked.

"I'm good. How're you feeling?" I realized I wanted her to really tell me.

I was feeling very pumped about Rome. But I knew things still weren't perfect.

"A little tired," she admitted. "But really good. What a trip, right?"

"Yeah, it was amazing."

Suddenly a kind of wave came over me. I felt a tear slide down my cheek.

"Oh, sweetie," she said, and she reached her hand across the aisle.

I smiled at her. I reached back across and held her hand lightly. We were almost home.

Is it crazy that I think I missed my board more than my bed when I was gone? Or more than my room? Mission Dolores? I definitely missed getting to zip around with Flint and J. It was so nice when we were able to get back to it.

"Rome was the bomb," Flint said. "I still can't believe that trip actually happened."

"I loved it," Jabari said. "I think I may apply to study abroad over there."

"Do not tell me that you just said 'study' when it's almost the first week of summer. I think you have been body-snatched by a zombie and replaced with a geeky old teacher."

"I didn't say I was studying now! I said I might want to go to school there *someday.*"

Flint worked this over in his head. He was probably thinking what I was—I'd hate it if we weren't all together.

"Well, I don't know if that's such a great idea, J. Like Abraha—um, like Dorothy said in *The Wizard of Oz,* 'There's no place like home.'"

Jabari smiled. "Well, that's true. And I don't think we have to decide for sure today."

We started scooting around in the parking lot, lining up for some tricks and some jumps. Then we heard a car pulling in. It was Big Anne.

Flint looked a little worried. Our parents never came over here unless it was for a PTA meeting or game. Or something else for school.

But she didn't look upset or mad. In fact, she was smiling super big. She rolled the window down.

"Get in!" she yelled.

Which we did. With a million questions.

"Not gonna tell you," and "You'll see," and "It's a surprise," she kept saying as she drove. And drove and drove. Until we passed the Ghirardelli store and saw Fisherman's Wharf up ahead. Big Anne maneuvered the big car into a space. We jumped out and looked around. Whatever the surprise was, we couldn't see it just yet.

"This way," she said and power-walked up onto the sidewalk.

We fell in beside her. This was a pretty cool spot, on a whole other side of the city from where we lived. Or even from Lands End. There were people selling flowers and jewelry. There was a man playing a guitar like a rock star. Another guy had spray-paint cans and blank canvasses. In just a few seconds, he sprayed around, grabbing all the different colors one right after the other. When he was done, there was an amazing picture of the Golden Gate Bridge, with shooting stars and crazy waves.

"Albie! Come on," Flint called.

I pulled myself away from the painter and jogged to catch up with them.

And then I heard it.

The harmonica, that bluesy tune we first heard so many months ago. Flint's and Jabari's eyes were as wide as mine. Big Anne's face looked like it might break in two, she was smiling so hard. We followed the sound closer and closer until we got up to Pier 39. And there, sitting on a bench outside, was Jazz Bonnie and the lion-dog, Clyde.

We ran up to them, whooping and hollering. I got there first and gave Jazz a huge hug. I moved away quickly so Flint and J could get a turn. I knelt down and petted Clyde. He stared at me with those awesome eyes. He looked great. And so did Jazz. He had on a clean shirt and new boots. His eyes were clear and happy.

"What're you doing here?" I asked. I didn't see Jazz's bags or food. He followed my eyes and seemed to get what I was looking for. He clasped his hands together and shook his head.

"I work here," he said, and he broke into a big grin.

"No *way*!"

We were all shouting over each other and clapping him on the back. This was truly awesome.

"But there's more," Big Anne said.

"Yes. Maybe the most important part! I also live here. Well, *we* live here. Well, actually, we live over there."

Jazz pointed to a big boat that was docked at the Pier. *Boat the Bay* was painted on the side.

"Clyde and I help to run the bay cruise," he said proudly. "And at night we clean up and stay on the boat. Come on! Let me show you."

It was totally great. Jazz was completely pumped. We all were. I could've never come up with this plan in a million years. I looked at Big Anne. I remembered that she'd written a column about the tours before. She must have helped swing this deal. Now she'd *really* have a great story to tell.

The sun beat down on us, but the air was cool. It felt really amazing, looking out at my old friends and my new friends and the water. It was crazy to think how life worked out sometimes. It sure could be terrible. But it sure could be great.

Maybe this summer would be the best yet. Maybe it would be harder than last year. There was no way to know for sure. All I could really know was today.

And today was a wonderful day.

A man jumps onto the boat's deck, smiling broadly. He is lean and strong and a hard worker. Three excited boys follow close behind him. A furry dog trots aboard last, sniffing the salty air with his big black nose. In the distance, the sound of laughing and music and honking sea lions almost drowns out the roar of the boat's motor.

There are no customers today; instead, the captain is running the route with the man and his friends, just for fun. They cut easily through the choppy water. Fisherman's Wharf gets smaller and smaller. The dog stretches out on the floorboards, and his long fur whips in the wind.

One of the boys settles in beside him and hugs the dog's golden, silky neck. The boat makes its way under the magnificent Golden Gate Bridge, then turns toward the Presidio. The boy bows his head into the dog's soft back like a prayer, then raises his face up to the sun. Its bright rays blanket him in warmth and in light. A sweet energy courses through his veins. What a gift, this life.

DISCUSSION QUESTIONS
FOR NOW AND AT THE HOUR

1. The title of the story references part of the Hail Mary prayer that Albert recites during a difficult time, emphasizing the present moment and also future experiences of joy, pain, and the end of life. How does Albert's past intersect with his current experiences? What things exist throughout all of time (past, present, and future) in the story? Is it easier for you to focus on the present, or to think about the future?

2. Foreshadowing gives clues and hints about something that is going to happen later in a story. Can you find examples of foreshadowing related to Mary's diagnosis, Albert's desire to help find a cure, and their pilgrimage to Rome? Were you expecting the things that ultimately happened?

3. Albert loves the freedom and adventure of skateboarding. How is this interest unusual given other aspects of his personality? What do we learn about his relationship to his mom through her

reactions to his skateboarding? Are there activities or interests that you use to relieve stress? What activities make you the happiest? Do you do them alone or with other people?

4. Early in the story when Pat confronts Albert and his friends, Albert thinks about what he has in common with the bully when he notices his army jacket. What does this say about Albert? Do you think he handled this situation well? How do his interactions with Pat change over the course of the story? How do they parallel how Albert is feeling about what's happening with his mom?

5. Albert and his friends have nicknames for each other, and some of the adults like Sister, Uncle Wood, and Big Anne also have nicknames. How are some of the names symbolically significant? What do you learn about the characters through their nicknames? If you have a nickname, how did you get it? Do you like it?

6. Albert's father, Pat's father, and Jazz Bonnie served in the military. What are special challenges that military families face? How did Jazz Bonnie's military experience continue to affect him even after he came home from Iraq? How does Albert feel when he wakes up on July 4? Is that how most Americans feel? Should it be?

7. Why do you think Albert decided to try to save the shark near the Cliff House? How did that event reappear in different forms throughout the story? Have you ever had a "save the shark" moment?

8. Trees are powerful symbols in this story. Why are they important to Albert? Find examples where trees are featured, and note what they represent in those parts of the story. What are some other objects, places, or events in the story that help to convey a larger meaning or significance?

9. Albert tries to control a lot of things: his emotions, his mom's experience, Jazz and Clyde's situation. What are different strategies he uses for maintaining control? Are they always healthy? What problems arise for Albert when he is engaged in this behavior? How does Albert's experience change this part of his personality?

10. The reader meets Albert before his mom's diagnosis. What was life like for his family before cancer? What are examples of good things and bad things prior to her illness? Describe some things that changed after she began treatment. What are examples of good things and bad things that happened when she was sick?

11. Having faith might be described as believing in something you cannot see. What role does faith play in Albert's experience? How would you

describe his faith journey––or the ways his faith changes or evolves––throughout the story?

12. Which relationships are most important to Albert? What are the different communities that show up to support his mom's fight against cancer? Do you believe it's possible to have meaningful connections with strangers? With animals? With nature? With art? Find examples of these kinds of bonds in the story. How do these connections––or the absence of them––change how we experience life?

13. Do you use social media? How was it useful to Albert and his family? How was it problematic? What lessons can you learn from Albert's experience on Twitter?

14. Albert and his mom go on a pilgrimage (a special journey) in search of a transformative change. Why do they go to Rome for their pilgrimage? How was Albert changed by the experience? Was the change that occurred the one he originally wanted?

15. Compare and contrast the opening and closing scenes of the story. How does each one make you feel? Imagine what might happen after this story ends for Albert and his friends, or for your favorite character.

ACKNOWLEDGMENTS

In *Now and at the Hour*, Mary says, "I'm so grateful for my life, this beautiful life. All I can see are my blessings." Those were the first lines penned for this novel, and the ones I feel most deeply about the evolution of a sentiment that became an idea, then a story, and finally a book I can now hold in my hands.

I remain thankful for the vivacious Sheri Gersin, the most adept people collector and connector I've ever met. She took such pleasure in her family, and cherished the time spent with Keith and Henry and Sam. Her big love for her life and the people in it inspired this story and is at its heart. I'm grateful she encouraged me to lift up the sustaining parts of some hard experiences.

Thank you to my family and friends for supporting my writing endeavors. Every time you asked about the book and cheered me on, you helped to make this possible. I'm grateful for my mother, Mary Murchison, who first introduced me to books as a child and who championed my passion to write one myself someday. Thank you for dusting off your English teacher's red pen in service to this story. I greatly appreciate the thoughtful enthusiasm of my father and stepmother, John and Gail Murchison. Thanks to my brother, John Murchison, for providing my first insight into the world of boys and the bonds of siblings; and to Meredith, Clara, Lilly, and

Garrett. To all of you, and to my extended family of in-laws, outlaws, aunts, uncles, and cousins: evidence of your warm presence in my life is immersed throughout the pages of this story.

I am forever indebted to folks who helped me start, pursue, and finish this project. Shout out to the Queens OCOM MA class of 2009 for planting early writing seeds, especially Ruth Baldrige, Kim Weller, Jason Fararooei, and Clint Patterson. Many thanks to Betsy Beaven Thorpe for helping to discern a plan; to Kim Wiley for keen insight and empowering instruction; and to the Dragonfly House Writers for valuable support and feedback. I am immensely grateful to Tyson Greene, Deborah Russo, and Angie Stofko for helping to rekindle that special kissy lip energy, so that this story could be a celebration.

To my faith family at Myers Park Presbyterian Church, thank you for being an enduring and centering presence in my life. You helped me find the living words, epitomized in the joyous Psalm 100.

To the many brave souls who helped with research for this book or who suffered through rough drafts and offered feedback, you are my heroes: Joanna Boyd Best, Scott Williams, Morgan Dow Cromwell, Brandon Vaden Janiak, Megan Fink Brevard, Olivia Patt, Alex Fleischli, Kimmery Martin, Tracy Curtis, Fletcher Curtis, Mary Murchison, Deborah Russo, Angie Stofko, Catherine Farley, Jason Fararooei, and my book club gals. Everything that is spot on is to their credit—all mistakes belong to me. Thanks to others who offered support along the way, including Ginger Wagoner, Lauri Eberhart, and Lance White.

Thank you to Dr. Atul Gawande for the book *Being Mortal*, and for sharing the poignant notion of "fighting for time now" at the Learning Society lecture at Queens University of Charlotte in February of 2016. I listened to you in that dark theatre with tears streaming down my face, and a missing piece of life's puzzle clicked into place.

To my fellow founding members of Writing Group, Ink: Kimmery Martin, Tracy Curtis, and Trish Rohr— you inspire me and make me brave, in writing and in life. I adore you and your fierce creations. Thank you for nurturing *Now* with your mad skills. A special shout out to Tracy for being the first to show me my name in print in a published book, and first to believe that I could get there myself the usual way.

To the team at Warren Publishing, you are brilliant and bring dreams to life. Thank you to Monika Dziamka and Melissa Long for your editorial assistance, and to Marcy Westphal for my beautiful cover. A very special thanks to Mindy Kuhn and Amy Ashby for wearing many hats at all times with unflappable grace, and for your unwavering support, patience, and expertise.

And finally, I happily acknowledge the three who prove that the greatest of these is love. To my sons, Will and Dillon Kercher, you are incredible human beings and I'm so proud to be your mom. Albert Davidson was created with great affection because, as I wrote him, I so often thought of you two. And to the rock and rock star of our family, Kent Kercher: you are the whole wide world. Thank you for buying my chairs.

ABOUT THE AUTHOR

BESS KERCHER indulged her love of stories at Davidson College, where she majored in English and dabbled in creative writing. She later graduated with an MA in organizational communication from Queens University of Charlotte, and began freelance writing shortly thereafter. She contributed to *The Charlotte Observer* online from 2013–2017 on their MomsCharlotte platform, authoring parenting essays and the blogs *Worst Mom Ever, Miracle on Curbstone Street, Mom and Pop, Because Friends, Team Mom,* and *A Few Good Moms: Can you handle the truth?* She once won a writing contest as a blogger for *skirt. Magazine* online (skirt!.com) and her prize was a copy of the book *My Formerly Hot Life.* The award seemed cruelly apropos, but still made her day ... because there's nothing like putting yourself out there and then feeling like someone gets you. She currently enjoys a cozy, lukewarm life in Charlotte, North Carolina with her husband, two sons, and family mascot/dog, Maddie.

CPSIA information can be obtained
at www.ICGtesting.com
Printed in the USA
JSHW031431300322
24413JS00003B/15